Catherine Hardin
D0094809

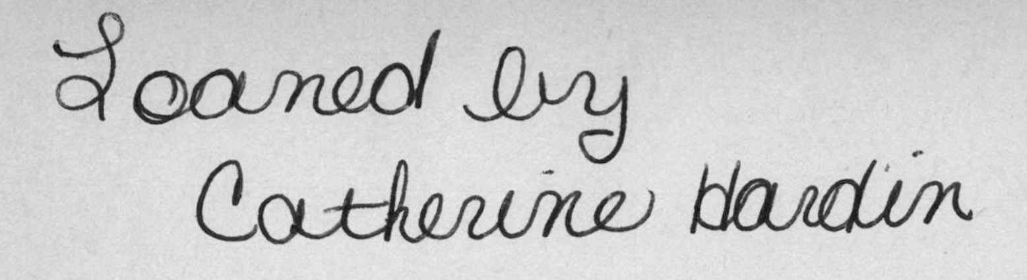

Robin Kane

Your

ROBIN KANE

Library

1 The Mystery
of the Blue Pelican

2 The Mystery
of the Phantom

THE MYSTERY OF THE BLUE PELICAN

by Eileen Hill

illustrated by
Sylvia Haggander

WHITMAN PUBLISHING COMPANY • Racine, Wisconsin

Racine, Wisconsin
Printed in the U.S.A. by
Western Printing and Lithographing Company

CONTENTS

1. *On Camera!*

ROBIN KANE, thirteen, slowly hung up the telephone receiver. She ran her tanned fingers through her shock of brown curls, her blue eyes wide with disbelief. Then, with a whoop she ran down the hall of her rambling home, calling at the top of her voice, "Mom! Kevin! Amy! Dad! Where *is* everybody?"

From outside, her mother's quiet voice answered, "On the patio—except Dad. He's in his studio. What is it?"

Robin stumbled down the step that led from the

big family room to the pool and stood breathless, her whole face shining. "You'll never in this world believe it!"

"Oh, Robin, shoot!" Kevin, her year-older brother lazily pulled dead leaves from the pool with a dip net. "I know one thing. Nobody's landed on Mars. Who were you talking to?"

"My best friend, Melinda Hunter, if you want to know, daughter of Mr. Maxfield Hunter, the big moving picture and television producer."

"Heck, we all know what Mindy's father does," Kevin said, and lowered himself into the water.

"Maybe so, but you don't know that his daughter's closest friend—me—*and* her brother Kevin, *and* her younger sister Amy are going to be in one of Mr. Hunter's pictures!"

Robin stood dramatically arranging the folds of an imaginary movie star's train as she awaited the reaction to her news.

"Gol!" Kevin exclaimed. "Honest on the square?"

"Are we going to Hollywood?" Amy asked, squeezing her cat Tig till he scratched and spit. "Mom, does she really mean it?"

Mrs. Kane stopped digging in the ground around

her roses and smiled. "I suppose she does, Sugar," she said. "I think you'd better tell us a little more about it, Robin."

"I haven't told you the most exciting part of all—" she began.

"Oh, stop stringing things out. You've made your entrance. Spill it!" Kevin said good-naturedly.

Robin gave him her best look of scorn, then the words burst out: "Moira Rafferty, the most famous girl actress in the world, is staying right there at Mindy's home!"

Amy squealed and threw her arms around Robin. "Moira Rafferty! I'm president of her fan club here in Pacific Point! Is she right here in our village? Clear from Ireland?"

"That's right, Sugar," Robin said and patted her little sister's head. "And I'll bet you'll have the first chance any fan club president ever had to act in a real live film."

"Don't you think you'd better start at the beginning?" Mrs. Kane asked. "I'm bursting with curiosity myself."

Mr. Kane slammed the door on his small studio cottage in the far rear of the yard and joined his family at the pool. Tramp, the lop-eared family mongrel, yipped at his heels in excitement.

"What's up?" Mr. Kane asked. "How come all the noise?"

"Oh, Daddy, Robin's just about to tell us. Listen, please. It's about Moira Rafferty and us!"

"Do tell!" Her father winked at Amy. "Moira Rafferty? Who is she?"

"Daddy!" Robin's voice was unbelieving.

"Oh, he's teasing," her mother said. "Don't you know your daddy's teasing voice? Speak up, Robin."

"Well, it's this: Mindy just telephoned to me to tell me that Moira and her father, Tim Rafferty, are staying at their home. They are both in Moira's new picture, *The Changeling,* and guess what!"

"For the ninety-ninth time, what?" Kevin asked, disgusted.

"Part of the picture is going to be made right here in Pacific Point, California, and some of the people in Pacific Point are going to be in it. Some of those people are us."

"Where do they have a studio in this town?" Kevin asked. "She's making the whole thing up."

"I am not! Didn't you ever hear of pictures

shot on location? Some of the action in this picture is going to be right up on Roberto Street. Some of it is going to be out at Rancho Lucia. The palominos will be in it there, mostly my darling Nugget." Robin stopped, put her hand over her mouth. "Someone else will ride him."

"Someone else always rides him in Mr. Hunter's pictures. That's why he keeps them at the ranch, all four palominos. That's why he bought the ranch. So there's nothing new about that." Kevin dried himself on a big beach towel, pulled his terry-cloth shirt on over his head. "Now do you think you could brief the Kane family on our part in this epic? I'll think it over and see if I can give them some of my talent and time."

"Listen to him!" Robin cried. "He's been to every Moira Rafferty picture that ever came to the Golden Bough. Three, four times, some of them. If he'll spend money on movies instead of saving for guitar strings or a new surfboard. . . ."

"Discussion time is up!" Mr. Kane announced. "Let's hear more about the Roberto Street episode in *The Changeling*."

"It isn't much of a part we'll play," Robin said,

subdued, "but it *is* in the picture. Moira is to turn the corner from the library, walk up Roberto Street to the record shop, open the door, and walk in. Inside is where the real part of the picture will be taken."

"And you think they can crowd all of us, the cast of the picture, the cameras, and everything into that little two-by-four record shop?" Kevin asked.

"Oh, we won't be in that part of it. We'll just be walking along the street as we always do. Amy will be riding her two-wheeler. Tramp will be with us. He always is. You and Mindy's brother Michael will stand on the corner and whistle at Moira as she goes by."

"Boy, I've whistled at her plenty on the screen!" Kevin admitted. "That's great, Robin. When do we start? Now?"

"The first thing tomorrow morning. At dawn, practically. Well, six thirty, anyway. We can watch all the preparation. The street's going to be roped off. All the big equipment will be here from Hollywood—golly!" The impact of the next morning's event seemed to hit Robin with reality all at once. Suddenly she sank down next to her mother on the stone bench at the side of the pool.

"I can see a ray of light in the whole business," Mr. Kane said. He filled his pipe and tamped down the tobacco. "If Mr. Hunter is starting to use you kids in his work you won't always be griping because I put you in my comic strip."

"There's a lot of difference," Robin said. "We'll act ourselves in the motion picture. In your 'Family Scene,' you just take what we do and let Fatso, Muggins, and Danny act instead of us."

"I like being Muggins," Amy said happily.

"I think I make a pretty good Danny," Kevin said.

"How'd you like to be Fatso in the strip?" Robin said. "Not much, I guess."

"Better hold back on the sodas, Sis," Kevin teased.

"Look who's talking! I'm *not* fat, am I, Daddy?"

"Not one bit, honey," her father said and started back to his studio. "It's just that you keep saying the darnedest things. Real smart, some of them. Some of them funny. What would I do without my family as inspiration?"

"I don't blame Robin at all. Try making me Fatso for once and see what happens," Mrs. Kane said, laughing. "Don't you have to get this week's strip into the mail, Toby? This afternoon?"

"Slave driver," he sighed. "Oh, all right. I'll make the four o'clock pickup at the post office. Don't worry. When do *I* meet this Moira Rafferty and her father?"

Robin snapped her fingers. "That's something else I had to tell you. After tomorrow's shooting she's coming back home with us. Mindy said so. If we'd like to have her come."

"Imagine that! If we'd like it!" Amy said dreamily. Her big brown eyes grew bigger in her oval face framed in long, straight golden hair. "Mom, can I wear my white organdy dress in the picture tomorrow?"

"May I," her mother corrected, and added, "To ride your bike?"

"Shorts for you and a T-shirt," Robin said decidedly.

"What'll you wear?" Amy asked, almost in tears.

"Same thing. Shorts. You, too, Kevin."

"I don't have anything else to wear even if I wanted to. I even go to church in shorts. And that suits me just fine."

"Mom?"

"Yes, Robin."

"Do you think we could have the Mexican tin lights hung around the patio for tomorrow when Moira comes? And maybe something other than hamburgers?"

"Mexican lights, yes. Anything but hamburgers, no. Wait and you'll see that I'm right. Moira is probably just like all the girls you know, and all the girls you know always want hamburgers."

"I know, but she's a movie actress!" Amy insisted.

"She's Irish, too, and who ever heard of hamburgers in Ireland?" Robin asked.

"I did and your daddy did when we were in Ireland last year. Everybody in the whole world, even in darkest Africa, eats hamburgers. All young people, anyway."

"In Africa cannibals may even make hamburgers out of—"

"That's enough, Kevin! That's quite enough. You finish getting the debris out of the pool. Then adjust the filter in the pool. If we're to have a guest tomorrow. . . ."

"I don't want a guest that badly—even her," Kevin protested. "What's Robin going to do?"

"I'm going to help Mom in the house."

"Work, work, work," Kevin said. "Why can't Mindy ask us to her house for a change? She has a yardman to do all the work; someone to cook—"

"That mausoleum?" Robin asked. "Who wants to go there?"

"You can think of a better word to use than mausoleum," her mother told Robin. "It's magnificent."

"Maybe so, but, Mom, you know as well as we do that nobody ever has any fun at the Hunters'. It's beautiful. It's colossal—"

Kevin snorted. "That's the way the movie ads describe movies."

"That's just what the Hunter house looks like—a set in the movies. Give me our big old shabby home every time," Robin said.

"Maybe we don't like to go there because Mindy's mom isn't there. She's dead," Amy said soberly.

"Oh, Sugar, that's exactly it," Robin said and put her arm around her mother. "It's our mom that Mindy and Michael love to see when they come here. Nobody cares over at their house, except maybe Manuela, their housekeeper. Their dad's too busy.

It will be wonderful to have Moira here."

"I just hope she turns out to be like she is in the movies," Kevin said. "If she does, she'll be okay. She's about Robin's age, so she should like the same things we like. The place where she lives in Ireland is on the ocean, and she probably likes swimming. Gee, she may even like sailing and surfing."

"You can't do all those things in one evening," his mother said, smiling. "I must get back to my work in the house. I don't know where this day has gone. It's nearly dinner time. Robin, come and help me, please."

"I'll go and straighten up our clubhouse," Amy said busily.

"Just keep away from my surfboard!" Kevin warned.

"And my water skis!" Robin called.

"Don't disturb Daddy at the other guesthouse, please," Mrs. Kane said.

"At least Mom said 'please,' " Amy reminded her brother and sister. "The Huddle belongs to all of us, and it's Mindy and Michael's clubhouse, too. I'm the one who always straightens it up. I'm the one who made your bed this morning, too, Robin. I always do, you know, at least most of the time."

"Gosh, Sugar, I'm sorry. I forgot it."

"Thanks, Sug, for keeping the Huddle neat," Kevin sang out. "Come on down to the beach with me, if you'll be a good little gremmie and just watch while I see if I can catch a wave. I fixed the filter, Mom. I'll get my board, Sugar."

"Well, now, that's more like it," Mrs. Kane said. "For a while I thought you'd turned into Muggins, Danny, and Fatso." She tied her apron around her trim waist, pushed back her dark hair, so much like Robin's. "Let's have an early dinner tonight. If you have to get up before six o'clock in the morning I know the groans and sighs I'll hear. It had better be early to bed tonight."

2. *Moira*

EARLY THE NEXT morning when Robin, Kevin, and Amy walked up to the village from their home near the beach they found the whole place bustling.

The sky was still pink over the Santa Lucia hills, and ribbons of fog clung to the tall pines and spreading cypresses. It would be another hour before the sun shone brightly, yet crowds of villagers had gathered all around the roped-off areas.

Police busily diverted traffic from the center of the village. All streets leading to the corner where the record shop stood were barricaded. Heavy trucks rolled down Ocean Avenue from the Los Angeles state highway—sound trucks, trucks loaded with camera equipment, portable dressing rooms. It wasn't long until the village was transformed.

On the street Robin spied Mr. Hunter, busily directing the placement of equipment. He saw her, too, and called to the guard, "Let the kids through, Bob." Then, as the trio walked importantly past the policeman at the corner of Roberto Street, Mr. Hunter added, "Go across the corner to the Cupboard, Robin. You'll find a lot of the extras in the cast at the long tables on the patio there. Some of them missed their morning coffee and are drinking it now. I'm glad you brought your bike, Amy. And there's Tramp. Good! I'll see you all later over there at the Cupboard. I don't think Mike and Mindy are there yet. Yes, here they come."

Amy ran to meet the Hunters, Tramp panting at her heels. "Where's Moira?" she asked.

"Getting her makeup on," Mindy said, "over there in that portable dressing room."

"Is she . . . ?"

"She's darling!" Mindy said breathlessly, her long,

wavy blond hair in disarray, for she had hurried. "She's the most natural person you could ever hope to see. I've met a lot of actresses in Daddy's company but she's . . . well, she's just like one of us. But you can see for yourself, for there she is."

Mindy waved to the girl who came down the steps from the truck. Her black hair hung smooth, uncurled and silky below her narrow shoulders. The slim, black-sheathed figure could have walked down the length of any *Rue de la Paix* dress shop in Paris. Her face, turned toward the waiting young people, was expressionless.

"Holy cow!" Kevin cried. "That's Moira Rafferty? You say she's just like one of us—with that face? She looks like a zombie from Zombieville. Jumpin' cats! Is that what I'm supposed to whistle at?"

"Oh, Kevin," Mindy said haughtily, her dark eyes snapping. "It's perfectly plain that you've never seen anyone who's been made up for the cameras."

"I guess I haven't, but golly, she doesn't even look like a human being—yellow paint on her face, and look at the way she walks!"

Mindy laughed. "In this picture, *The Changeling,* she plays two parts. In one of them she's a wholesome outdoors girl. In the other part she's sophisticated and mean. That's the one she is today."

"I'll say she looks the part. Why didn't she even wave to you?"

"She has to keep in character. Please, please, Kevin, wait till the shooting is over. Then you'll see what she's really like. Are we going to your house afterward, Robin?"

"Yes," said Robin slowly, her eyes glued to the slender, sauntering "changeling." "Heavens, do we all have to have that glop on our faces?"

"No. It's just because Moira is to have some shots made inside the record shop under lights. Outside, they'll shoot her from the distance as they will us. We don't need makeup for that. Say, how'd you like to go over to the makeup truck and see what you'd look like under the lights with just your natural faces? I know Daddy won't mind because there'll be time before the action really starts."

"I'd love it," Robin said. "Come on, Kevin, Amy."

"Skip it," Kevin answered. "I'll take your word for what it looks like. I'll stay here with Mike. This is where we're supposed to stand and whistle. Boy, that Moira is a sellout!"

"You'll eat those words," Mindy said, laughing. "You'll most certainly eat those words."

Inside the portable dressing room the lights blazed. Mindy explained to the makeup man what she wanted, and he seated Robin in a chair before the mirror. What she saw there almost made her jump from her seat. "I'm the purple people-eater!" she cried. "Look at me, Amy! Wheeew!"

Robin's eyebrows had faded from sight. Her big blue eyes were colorless, and as flat as dishwater. Her chin receded. Her narrow patrician nose—her proudest feature—seemed thick and short, and the thin sprinkling of freckles stood out like polka dots. The dimple in her cheek became an ugly hole, and her mouth was a wan slash in an expressionless face.

"Do I honestly look like that? Amy's afraid of me. Is that the way people see me?"

"No, honey," the makeup man said. "I'll fade the lights to normal for a minute and you'll see yourself as you look in daylight. When the strong lights are on, every feature has to be accented, shadowed, highly colored. If I had time I'd show you the makeup that would be needed then."

"You don't need to. I just saw Moira Rafferty.

It's ghastly. Kevin will never believe us when we tell him how I looked. What do we do now?"

Mindy held up her hand. "Listen!"

A loudspeaker crackled and a voice called out, "Extras! Places, please!"

"That's us," Mindy said. "Call Tramp, please, Amy. Come on, Robin. We have to hustle around the corner and get ready to walk down the street slowly. Amy, where's your bike?"

"I parked it at the corner. Where shall I ride?"

"Right behind Robin and me. Daddy said for us to walk slowly down the street, stopping now and then as though looking in the windows. Then we're supposed to walk on past the record shop where Moira will be. Ready?"

They had walked about half the length of the block when Mr. Hunter called, "Cut! Try it again!"

"What went wrong?" Robin asked.

"Half a dozen things might have happened. Oh, it must have been Amy. Are you all right, Sugar?"

"I fell off my bike, that's what!" Amy said. "I spoiled the whole picture."

"Did it hurt you?" Robin asked. She lifted the fallen bike quickly and grabbed her little sister's hand, looking her over with an anxious eye.

"I'm not hurt. I'm just mad. I *never* fall off. Now everything's spoiled."

"No, it isn't at all," Mindy said quickly. "I've never known my daddy to be satisfied with a first take. Let's try it again now. The camera's waiting."

This time when they walked down the street they met a little boy about seven years old holding tightly to the hand of a shabbily dressed man. "Maybe they're in the scene," Robin thought. As the girls passed, the boy stopped, knelt on the ground to pet Tramp who wagged his whole brown and white body happily.

Robin could see the cameraman gesturing wildly, evidently urging the man to keep going. Then she saw Mr. Hunter answer him by forming the letter O with his forefinger and thumb. Mindy whispered, "I don't think they're supposed to be in the picture, but I guess Daddy wants the camera to catch it. He signaled *okay*. Go on just acting naturally. You, too, Amy."

She needn't have bothered about Amy. She was entirely absorbed in the boy and Tramp.

"My daddy just met me at the bus," the boy told

her. "My daddy's a soldier."

"Not just now I'm not," the man said and glanced quickly at the two older girls. "I've been out of the service a while. All I want is to find a decent job to take care of my kid. Come on, Jeff."

Robin was speechless. Mindy with the poise of a seasoned actress told the man she hoped he would find work, said good-bye to the boy, and motioned to Amy to remount her bike. All the time the cameras kept rolling.

"We'll print that," Mindy's father called through his megaphone. "It's a nice bit of atmosphere. Good work, girls! That's all for the day. Tell Mike and Kevin, too, that they're free."

"That little boy liked Tramp," Amy said. "Is that all we get to do in the picture? Where's Moira?"

"That's all we do today, Sugar," Mindy said. "It didn't take long, did it? Just about an hour."

"It seemed forever to me," Robin said. "They rehearsed Moira over and over. Do they always take that much time? I'd think they'd never finish a picture."

Mindy laughed. "The part we were in will only show about one minute on the screen. It usually takes a whole day's shooting for only a couple of minutes of finished film."

"Heavens, no wonder it costs so much money."

"Where's Moira?" Amy asked again.

"In the dressing room taking off her makeup and changing her dress, I guess. Wasn't it fun?" Mindy asked.

Amy hung her head.

Robin looked dubious. "Maybe we thought it would be different," she said slowly. "Don't you think we'd better go to your house instead, Mindy? She'll probably think we're a bunch of beatniks at our house. You know . . . hamburgers and all."

"Now you listen to me," Mindy began, "both of you. I told you she's wonderful."

"That's what I've been trying to tell Kev." Michael's freckled face reddened to the top of his sandy crew cut. "All the time we were over there at the Cupboard. He didn't give a very convincing whistle when Moira went by."

"Somebody taking my name in vain?" A laughing girl crowded into the circle between Mindy and Robin. Her long black hair was held back with a blue headband that matched her faded T-shirt and blue shorts. She looked around with a smile.

Kevin took one look and the whistle he shrilled was genuine.

"Are *you* Moira?" Robin asked, wide-eyed.

"Yes. Wasn't I poisonous in that part? Didn't you hate me? That's the effect I had to try for. Mindy, can we go somewhere else? Didn't you say we were going to Robin's house? Please! If you only knew how I've been looking forward to it. You're Amy, aren't you, honey? You're the picture of my own little sister Deirdre. I saw you, Kevin, when I passed you and Mike on the street. Sure, and you looked as though you wouldn't give me the back of your hand!"

Moira's blue eyes were mischievous. Kevin snapped his fingers and started up the street. Laughing, chattering, they all found Michael's old station wagon in front of the library.

"I'll take you home," he told them. "Then I have to go out to the ranch on some business for Dad. I'll pick you up later."

"Can't you even wait for a hamburger?" Robin asked as they started off. "You'll starve, Michael."

"Imagine Mamacita or José out at the ranch

letting anyone starve!" Michael laughed. "Don't worry, Robin. Want to come along, Kev?"

Kevin glanced shyly at Moira. "Not a chance," he said firmly.

"See you around eight, then," Michael said a little later as he stopped to let them off at the Kane's gate.

Out at the pool Moira kicked off her sandals and dabbled her feet delightedly in the water. Amy's big cat stretched lazily, then walked daintily into the Irish girl's lap, curled up and purred. Kevin came running from the house in swim trunks, waved to the girls, then bounded out onto the diving board and sliced the water gracefully with his tanned length.

Mr. and Mrs. Kane wheeled the grill to the edge of the patio and started to light the heaped charcoal.

Robin and Amy spread the long redwood table with a plastic cloth. Mindy followed with paper plates.

"There, there now," Moira called and dumped the surprised black cat on the ground. "I want to help, too. I want to do my share. What may I do, Mrs. Kane?"

"You shouldn't do anything," Mindy said. "We planned it for you."

"You want me to sit here like a grand lady?" Moira's eyes danced. "You should let my mother hear that, or my daddo. In my home in County Kerry everyone helps. If we don't we may feel the touch of a willow switch on our legs."

Amy gasped. "Do you really have to help at home just like us?"

"Indeed I do, lamb. It's this way. There are eight of us in the family. I'm third from the top. We've each of us a job to do, or how else would my mother get anything done? It's hard on her when my daddo and I have to travel to make a picture . . . like now. Every day of my life I have nine beds to make up when I'm home, and that's the truth."

"Oh, Moira, wait till I tell the girls in our fan club," Amy said, fascinated. "Some of them were watching on Roberto Street today. They probably all think you're like *that* girl."

"They'd have a fan club for a creature like that? I'll never believe it."

"I guess I mean they'd think you have servants and everything," Amy said, embarrassed.

"We've Meg who comes once a week to iron and do the worst of the scrubbing," Moira said. "With three big girls like my sisters and me who needs servants?"

She poured milk from a pottery jug and set the full glasses to the right of the plates. "I love it here! The sound of the waves down there on the beach. They're wild on the Kerry coast. The smell of the pine trees. You should walk through the forest of them on the rise to McGillicuddy's reeks!" Her dreamy look faded as she sniffed the smoke from the grill. "Mmmm! There's nothing so good as a hamburger. You'll see the pig I'll be when we're at the table."

Moira was as good as her word. Time after time the salad bowl was passed to her. She stopped counting hamburgers and pickles. When the big meringue Mrs. Kane had baked and filled with peach ice cream was brought in, the young Irish girl moaned and said, "I'm like the boy from Connemora at Christmas time when the plum pudding came. I can chew but I can't swallow."

After supper was over, Moira helped clear the table. She carried paper plates to the huge burner back near the Huddle and Mr. Kane's studio. She gathered knives and forks and spoons and carried them to the dishwasher in the kitchen. In no time at all, darkness came and with it fog dimming the moon over the hills.

When Michael came back from the ranch to take the girls home, he found Moira and Amy snuggled close together on a stone bench by the pool. Tramp sat beside them, and Moira gently pulled his ears. Across the pool Kevin's guitar tinkled, and Robin and Mindy hummed half under their breaths. Fragrant smoke came from Mr. Kane's pipe as he stretched in the redwood chaise longue by the pool's side.

"You're just in time for a Coke, Michael," Mrs. Kane called from the kitchen step. "In time, too, to help me with this tray. You aren't going to break things up this early, are you?"

"I guess the news I have to tell will break things up," Michael said soberly, his kindly face troubled. "You're not going to like it a bit, Robin. I hate most of all to tell *you*. Nugget's gone. Disappeared from the corral this afternoon."

"Stolen?" Robin couldn't believe her ears. "Someone stole Nugget? Oh, no, no, no, Michael. No!"

"It's true," Michael said sadly. "He's gone. We don't know where. In broad daylight, too."

"Just gone?" Robin was near tears. "Wasn't there any clue at all? He couldn't have wandered away."

"He didn't. The corral gate was closed. The cowboys were out on the range. José was mending a fence over the hill. Mamacita and Felipe were taking a siesta."

"Did you tell Daddy?" Mindy asked, her arm around Robin.

"I called him right away. He and Mr. Rafferty went out to the ranch. Dad said he'd call the sheriff, but that there wasn't any use to try and do anything more tonight. Nobody could find anything in those hills after dark."

"How could he get away without *any* trace?" Robin asked. "Without any clue whatever?"

"Well, unless you'd call a scrawl on the corral fence a clue," Michael said. "José said it wasn't there before. He was sure of that. It was a rough blue outline of a bird—a pelican."

"A blue pelican," Robin said thoughtfully, sadly. "A blue pelican."

3. *Searching*

THAT NIGHT Robin tossed restlessly. Dreams of Nugget stirred her sleep—Nugget, with his beautiful golden coat, his silky mane and tail. Once she wakened sharply, certain she had felt his soft nose nuzzling her shoulder. He was such a dear, dear horse.

When day finally shone through the organdy-curtained window, her pillow was damp with tears. Quickly, before anyone else stirred, she hurried into dark green shorts and a sleeveless cotton shirt. Michael had said he would stop for her with Mindy when he took Moira to the ranch for the day's shooting.

In the bathroom she ran a damp comb through her curls, smiling suddenly as she remembered her mirrored goon face under the lights the day before. Then she slipped softly down the hall from her bedroom to the tiled kitchen.

Kevin heard her as she passed his room and soon joined her. Their mom always organized the food for breakfast the night before and left a menu on the counter. Robin poured cereal into bowls and then squeezed orange juice while Kevin reached into the refrigerator for cold milk and poured it into their glasses.

"Mike'll be here before long," Kevin said. "Boy, movie people sure get going before dawn, don't they?"

Robin didn't answer. She lifted her glass of milk and then sat thoughtfully looking off into space.

"You're worried about Nugget," Kevin said.

"Oh, I *am*. I can't bear to think that some wicked person is being cruel to him. If someone just spoke softly to him he'd probably go off with the person, he's so trusting. Where can he be?"

"I don't know, Sis, but I'll tell you this much:

The sheriff will find him, you can bet on that. I'd hate to have Sheriff Jackson looking for me. Why did they have to pick on Nugget, do you suppose?"

"Because he's the most beautiful, and the gentlest. Kevin, they just *have* to find him."

"Cheer up; maybe he'll be back when we get out to the ranch. Horse stealers get scared sometimes when they think there's a posse after them—there's Mike, anyway, and Mindy and Moira. Let's get going. Mom knows where we'll be."

Mike guided the wagon out of Pacific Point, around the winding road that skirted the ocean. Great waves rolled in from the fog-wrapped ocean and beat themselves into ripples and foam on the sandy beach. They went past the marina at Monteleone, with its white-sailed boats bobbing at their moorings. Then they turned south to the foothills of the Santa Lucia Mountains and the San Antonio River valley.

Moira's black hair was braided in two hoydenish pigtails for the other changeling she was to play today at Rancho Lucia. Her fair skin with pink, wind-whipped cheeks was not yet marred with the thick makeup. Her Irish blue eyes were serious, for she seemed to sense the anxiety of her newfound friends over the big golden horse.

"I've a mare at home," she said. "Well, she's not exactly mine, for all of us ride her. She knows me, though, the little black beauty. I think she even knows when I have to go away from home. I can tell how you feel, Robin—how you all feel. I've a queer thought, though. The Irish call it second sight. I'm sure you'll be getting your Nugget back."

"Oh, do you think you're right?" Robin asked, her eyes brightening. "Do you really truly, Moira?"

"That I do."

The road left the highway and began to wind in among the foothills. Far in the background they could see the first green glint of the Rancho Lucia pasture. Then the weathered corral fence came into view and beyond it the straggling adobe ranch house itself. There were moving-picture trucks, too, waiting, circling the barns, bunkhouse, and ranch house like covered wagons in a western movie.

Men in dark glasses were everywhere. They were spreading wires, stepping off distances, adjusting cameras, calling out orders. Chickens and ducks squawked and ran to and fro in the yard.

Two years before, Mindy's father had bought the

ranch from Manuela, now the Hunters' housekeeper. It had been in her family for generations. One of her ancestors had settled there under a grant from the king of Spain. The family had raised cattle and planted the valley fields in corn and grapes.

Gradually, one by one, the men who worked the soil had died or moved off to San Francisco, Sacramento, or Los Angeles. Their portraits and those of their wives still hung in faded stiffness in the big living room of the ranch. The massive, dark, homemade furniture was just as it had been when Manuela, the last of her line, decided to sell the ranch and go to keep house for the Hunters.

The adobe house itself, built U-shaped around a wide-spreading live oak, had grown with the generations that had known it. An ell branched off one way; a room projected in another direction. Wandering, shabby, not too polished, the house straggled hospitably over a quarter acre of ground. Inside the house, high-posted carved beds offered rest to any of Mr. Hunter's family or friends. The dining room sent out the welcoming fragrance of *frijoles* hot with chili peppers, *tacos* bursting with spiced seasoned meat, and juicy dried peach pies.

José, a *vaquero* who had grown up here, now old, but efficient, managed the ranch. Mamacita, his wife, kept house indifferently and lazily, and cooked marvelously for José, their orphan grandson Felipe, and herself. The cowboys at the bunkhouse had their own cook.

Perro, Felipe's big shepherd dog could be found —when he wasn't off herding cattle with the *vaqueros*—lying in the dust in a tangle of honeysuckle and jasmine vines near the kitchen porch.

After Michael had parked the station wagon, Moira went to find Mr. Hunter and the makeup man to get ready for the day's work. Michael and Kevin went off to the bunkhouse with Felipe and Perro tagging at their heels. Robin and Mindy followed the overgrown dirt path to the porch.

On the sloping veranda Mamacita sat serenely calm in all the confusion and noise, her pudgy hands folded over her fat stomach, rocking back and forth.

"Buenas dias," she said. Robin and Mindy returned her greeting, Robin's eyes searching beyond her to find José.

When he heard her voice he came out of the house. *"Amigicita!"* he cried. "The horse! You come because he is lost. How it happened I know not. *Senorita* Melinda, I tell your father I do not know. Nugget vanish just like that!" The old *vaquero* snapped his fingers and threw his arms into the air. "Felipe, he see nobody. Mamacita, whose ears are sharp as the bird's, she hear no one. I don't know how it happened unless . . . *magia negre!"* He said the words softly and fearfully.

"It *is* black magic, José," Robin said sadly. "Where is the mark you found on the corral?"

"Come, I show you." José beckoned and the two girls followed.

Outside, Moira, busy with a member of the cast, mounted another of the four palominos, Sutter's Gold. Nugget would have been in the picture with Moira instead, Robin thought sadly as she stopped at the fence with José. In blue chalk a childish scrawl outlined a pouch-throated pelican in flight. It was a crude drawing on the rough wood.

"Are you sure Felipe didn't draw this?" Robin asked, tracing the bird's body with her finger.

"Felipe, no," José answered. "Felipe, he ride the range with the *vaqueros* yesterday, away . . . over there." He pointed to the far pasture where white-faced Hereford cattle grazed and young calves kicked up their heels under the shelter of cottonwoods and willows. A slim stream sparkled in the sunlight as it trickled through the pasture from the hills. "No, *amigicita,*" José answered sadly. "It was no human thing that made this mark. It was *magia negre!*"

Mindy saw the look of horror on Robin's face and changed the subject abruptly. "Has Sheriff Jackson been here this morning?" she asked.

"Si, senorita."

"What did he say?"

"He took two men with him. They walked all over the corral. They went into the house. Why?" José spread his arms wide, hunched his shoulders. "Did Nugget live in the house? Bah!" He turned to Robin. "Do you know what he did then, *senorita?*"

Robin shook her head. "No, tell us."

"He ride off *that* way with his men." José motioned down the road that led to Monteleone. "A thief does not hide a horse in a city. He does not take him to the ocean. Where does he take him?" José wet his thumb and gestured toward the far Santa Lucia Mountains. "There!" he said dramatically.

"Sheriff Jackson is a very capable man," Mindy said slowly. "Daddy trusts him completely. He always finds the man he's after. You know that, José."

"So?" José raised his eyebrows. "After how many months? What will the horse look like at the end of many months? Will his long tail be chopped off? Will they feed him the sweet alfalfa? There, there, *amigicita,* don't cry."

Robin put her head down on the top rail of the corral. She wasn't crying. She was thinking.

Nugget *had* to be found right away. Nobody had ever been unkind to him, she thought to herself. He'll die if anyone is cruel to him. His beautiful tail cropped? No! His sleek coat muddied and rough? No! His way of hunting with a moist nose in her hand for sugar. The way he nodded his head when she taught him to count.

Eyes blazing, Robin whirled around. "I'm going out to look for Nugget myself. If he's any place in the hills and I call to him, he'll hear my voice and answer me. He wouldn't do that for Sheriff Jackson."

Old José laughed. *"Very* good, *amigicita,* little owl. You go, too?" he asked Mindy.

"Of course!" Mindy said excitedly. "Moira will be sick 'cause she can't go with us. Better not tell anyone we're going, José. We'll be back in a few hours and they won't even be through with the shooting."

"They might," José said and showed the girls the dark clouds gathering on the horizon. "If the rain comes, right back you come, *senoritas!* You mind José, hear?"

"We hear," Robin said, "but you know how it is in northern California in the summertime. It can look dark as night and we won't get a drop. Anyway, Kevin and Michael will go with us, I know."

"Not now, *senorita.* They get chaps from the *vaqueros* to be in picture. 'Extras,' they call it, extra *vaqueros,* see?"

"Well, then, we'll go by ourselves. What horses shall we take, Mindy?"

"José will tell us."

"I get the ponies. You go to the barn, get saddles."

"We'll get some sandwiches to take with us, first," Mindy said.

Out in the kitchen the two girls packed a small sack to throw over Robin's saddle—hasty sandwiches of cold *tacos* with mashed *frijoles* between them. Both girls filled their canteens with water, then went down to the barn.

The big old stable smelled of sweat-stained horse blankets and liniment. On its rough walls hung saddles and bridles. A shelf spilled worn currycombs, cans of yellow soap, fly-spray bottles, and a tangled litter of tools and polish boxes.

Robin went to the hook where Nugget's old-fashioned saddle hung, with its short stirrups and ornamental leather *tapideros*. She ran her hand lovingly over the bridle and put her head, for a moment, close to the Spanish saddle horn. Dear Nugget. Her head flew up. "I'll find you, Nugget," she promised under her breath. "Just be patient, for I'll find you."

When José came with the two cow ponies, the girls met him at the barn door with the light saddles. He handed the reins to Mindy and Robin, then brought out two old faded Navajo blankets folded square. He put these on the ponies, then the saddles, then busied himself with cinches, buckles, and bridles. As he tightened a strap on one of the pack ponies it shied nervously. The girls heard flying footsteps coming down the hard-packed mud path to the barn. It was Moira.

"What are you doing here?" Mindy asked. "Aren't you supposed to be back there where they're shooting?"

"I sneaked away," Moira answered breathlessly. "I saw José take the ponies from the corral and I thought I knew what that meant. Now I'm sure. But you can't go. They need you for extras. They're counting on both of you."

"I'm sorry," Robin said. "We're going to see if we can find where Nugget was taken."

"Heavens!" Mindy said. "Daddy won't like it."

"*You* understand, don't you, Moira?" Robin begged.

"Of course I understand, Robin. I daren't stay away longer or I'd go with you. What I'd give for a sprint over the heath with this one!" She reached on tiptoe to hug the spotted pony and tangle her fingers in his red-brown mane. "You're the dear one, indeed," she said lovingly. "I'll be going back," she told the girls, "but my heart will be right with you!"

"Here now, little one," José said and held the stirrup out for Robin's foot. "Up you go, *amigicita!*"

Robin threw her leg over the saddle, sat with shoulders back, head up, and her knees gripping hard against the pony's flanks.

Mindy mounted. Both girls chirruped and touched their heels to their ponies' sides. They broke from a sedate walk into a lively canter, and off they went along the trail to the hills, manes and tails flying.

Across the flat country the girls rode, and up a worn trail that led deeper and deeper into the wooded mountains.

On the rise before the road dipped into a canyon, Robin looked back.

Cameras still ground out footage for *The Changeling*. In a corner of the corral three palominos huddled waiting to be needed again—Sutter's Gold, Lucky, and shimmering Sunshine. One golden horse was missing—Nugget.

Robin took her hand from the braided leather rein and ran her fingers through her brown curls. "Let's go, Mindy," she said. "Let's go and bring Nugget back where he belongs!"

4. *Nugget! Nugget!*

GLORY, LISTEN to the stillness!" Robin said when they had been riding a while. "Nothing but the clink of the ponies' shoes on the trail! Say something, Mindy!"

"I'm thinking, and I'm watching, too." Mindy pulled her pony up short with a firm hand on his reins and soft steady words of encouragement. "Just look down below you, Robin, and for heaven's sake —oh! Do watch where you're going. Every time I ride this road I'm scared. Nothing way down there but boulders and the river rushing through the canyon! How can you be so confident?"

"I trust my pony." Robin stroked his slender neck gently. "Why do you suppose José gave you Seguro to ride, and me, Bueno? He certainly didn't give those names to the ponies for nothing. Seguro . . . 'dependable.' Bueno . . . 'good.' What are you laughing at, Mindy?"

"I'm laughing at your knowledge of Spanish, or José's lack of knowledge of English. My pony's name is not Seguro, but Sugar, and that's quite a different thing. Felipe named him after Amy. He adores her. Felipe always gets to name the horses that are broken and trained as cow ponies."

"Cheer up, in another hundred years I may learn," Robin answered, smiling. "I think I remember now that Amy did say one of the ponies had her name. . . . Isn't this a mess we've gotten into?"

All the prickly bushes in California seemed to have clumped together in the mass of growth ahead of them, wild lilac, manzanita, chaparral, scrub oak. The trail had all but disappeared. It was almost dark, too, and airless. A weird light came through the dense pines.

Robin dropped from her pony's back and pushed

ahead through the undergrowth, leading him. Mindy followed with Sugar.

A large deer ran out of the thicket followed by a slender doe. For an instant they stopped, heads up, then bounded away.

Robin's eyes grew misty and round. She stood motionless, watching. "It was beautiful. I love every living animal." Still filled with the wonder of the wild country and its creatures she shouldered her way down the trail, parting the bushes for her pony to follow. As she walked she called . . . gently at first, then loud and clear, "Nugget! Nugget! Where are you, Nugget? Answer me, Nugget!"

Only the echo of her voice came back. That and a rustling of leaves and the measured breathing of the ponies as they clop-clopped along the rocky path.

Once through the thicket, Robin mounted Bueno and the girls rode on. High above them on an old oak tree, they saw a grown-over Indian blaze, a cross cut into the bark.

"The Indians made a cross like that when a man was killed," Mindy said. "José told me."

"Mission Indians from San Carlos Borromeo used to call these hills and canyons their own," Robin said thoughtfully. "Father Dieudonne at Monteleone told me that. No one knows where they have gone now. They just died away or disappeared. He told me stories of Vasquez, the bandit, too. Did you ever hear of him?"

"Only his name. I guess we don't have to worry about him now, though, because he lived so many years ago, didn't he?"

"Yes, and he robbed the rich to give money to the poor, as Robin Hood did. He never harmed poor people. Many a large family found a fat purse on the table after Vasquez had passed by. Father Dieudonne told me that, too."

"I wish he'd tell us where we might find Nugget," Mindy answered sadly. "You've called him and called him."

"I know it. Oh, Mindy, where do you think he can be? This is the only trail through the woods that a thief could have taken with him. There isn't another way in the foothills any place near here. Don't you think that by this time we'd have seen some sign of him? It's a sure thing nobody's been through this thorny brush lately."

The trail widened and the two girls rode abreast.

Suddenly Robin reined her pony so abruptly that he almost stood on his hind feet. When he came down she reached frantically for a sprig of thorn tangled in Bueno's mane. "Do you see this?" she shouted to Mindy. Two or three long hairs had caught on the thorns. Long silver hairs. "Someone has gone through here, and with Nugget."

Without waiting for Mindy to say a word, she pressed her knees against Bueno's sleek side and was off. "Nugget!" she called at the top of her voice. "Nugget! Nugget!"

Only the wind answered.

It was a rising wind that had crept up the mountains without warning and now blew moist and cold through the thick woods.

"It's the storm!" Mindy cried. "José warned us. We must go back, Robin. Just look at that sky! I've never seen such black clouds. We promised José we'd turn back if a storm came up. We have to go, Robin."

"Now? Now that I know Nugget's near? Never!"

"Nugget could have been taken over this trail hours and hours ago. Whoever took him has had at least eight hours' start. He disappeared yesterday, you know. Besides, we promised José."

"We didn't promise, Mindy. We only listened to him when he warned us. I just *have* to find Nugget. He doesn't like storms."

"Neither do I. For heaven's sake have some sense. . . . *Do!* Now that we know Nugget's been over this trail it can't be too hard for the sheriff to trace him. Let's go back, please, before the storm breaks."

"You go back. I won't. I've seen clouds a lot blacker than this, and they didn't mean a thing. Oh, come with me, Mindy. If you don't I just have to go on by myself. My horse is ahead of us, somewhere. . . . Yes, I know Nugget isn't *my* horse. He belongs to Rancho Lucia and your father, but if love could make him mine, he's mine. I'm not going to desert him now. You love Nugget, too, don't you?"

"Of course I do. I don't want to risk my life in a cloudburst, though, especially when Nugget's nowhere around here. I can be sensible and still love him."

Robin turned a tragic face to her friend. "I can't. I just can't be sensible when I know that Nugget's lost."

"Do this, at least," Mindy said patiently. "Do you see that opening in the trees ahead of us? It's a mesa

—Mesa Aguidera—a good-sized one. You must remember it. The stream is narrow there, and down a little way there's a clump of willows and alders. Let's try and leave our ponies there for shelter when the worst of the storm comes. It's going to pour. Take my word for it."

"Can't we stay right here where we are, under the trees on the trail?"

"No. Ride on, Robin. There's a sort of a cave at the edge of the mesa. A shelf of rocks. If we hurry we can leave the ponies tied under the trees and run for cover in the cave. It's lucky José put halters under their bridles."

"Just so you don't turn back. I couldn't do that," Robin said and followed Mindy.

At the far end of the mesa near the spring they led their ponies into the grove. Selecting long, low-hanging branches, they tied the shank ropes securely so they wouldn't slide down the limbs. While they did this they spoke softly to Bueno and Sugar, telling them what they were doing.

Huge drops of water were falling as the two girls ran for the recess in the rocks at the other end.

Then the storm broke in fury. Branches of thick

pines back in the forest groaned and bent as the wind tore through. Close on the wind, blinding sheets of water followed, gale-driven.

Back under the rock shelf, Robin put her hands over her eyes and moaned, "Nugget's out in this storm someplace. He doesn't even know we're trying to find him."

"Bueno and Sugar are in the storm, too; don't forget that," Mindy reminded her. "You don't seem to worry about them. Nugget has sense enough to get in out of the rain."

"He does if someone leads him. Even if you think I don't, I do worry about our ponies, too. They ride the range, though, in all kinds of weather. Besides, we're right here with them. Maybe someone who doesn't care anything about Nugget is with him. He's sort of special, Nugget is."

"I love him, too. I love all our palominos."

"I know you do, Mindy, but—listen . . . you're my best friend, aren't you?"

"I hope so."

"Well, Nugget's my best horse. No one understands me the way he does when I talk to him."

"You think so much of animals, Robin, why don't

you study veterinary medicine when you go to college? All you've ever talked about is being a special agent someday."

"No, I still want to be an agent. More than ever. Then I can see that people who steal animals are punished. I think it's just as big a crime to steal an animal as it is to steal a person."

"I hope the judge feels the same way."

"When I get older maybe I can try to get that kind of a law passed. Do you think the rain is letting up a little?"

"It isn't blowing so hard. I know that. Let's go to the opening and see what's happening."

Outside, the air had brightened, cleared a little. Black clouds hurried down into the plains below toward the Rancho Lucia. That would mean the end of the day's work on *The Changeling*.

"We can leave here now," Robin said. "There'll be at least another hour to hunt for Nugget before we have to start back to the ranch."

She took Mindy's hand and they stooped to go under the shelf of rock. Then, suddenly, as the level ground in front of her came into view, Robin held her finger to her lips. Down the wooded trail she heard the sound of horse's hoofs. Nearer. Nearer. Sloshing over the wet ground.

"It's someone from the ranch looking for . . ." Mindy started to say. Her voice faltered for Robin's hand closed tightly over her mouth.

"Shhh!" she warned. "Get back into that pocket in the opening! I think it may be the thief."

Steadily the hoofs plodded nearer. Robin's white, frightened face peered from a tangle of vines. Her heart thumped wildly.

Nearer. Nearer. Nearer.

From around the turn a horseman rode into view. Stiff with fear, Robin saw a dark, wispy moustache, cruel cold eyes, and a crooked mouth gashed across an evil face. He rode so near the girls that the leather *tapideros* swinging from his stirrups brushed the vines and sent a spray of raindrops across Robin's eyes.

"It's *El Gato* . . . The Cat!" she gasped.

"Are you sure? How do you know?" Mindy moaned.

"I'm sure. I saw his picture in the paper just last week. He's the leader of a gang of cattle rustlers. He's one of the men most wanted by the F.B.I."

Terrified, they watched El Gato dismount a few yards from their hiding place. His horse's mouth foamed from the cruelly tight bit. Robin's hand tightened on Mindy's with anger at the man's inhumanity.

Without a word to his animal he tied it, short-reined, to a scrub oak. Then he pulled a bag of tobacco and some paper from the pocket of his black shirt and silently rolled a cigarette. His cold eyes narrowed on the trail he had just passed over.

Another man appeared.

"Whatcha stoppin' here for, El Gato?" the newcomer asked, slouching in his saddle. "The critters will be millin' around down where the trucks are. We shoulda gone the low wide road with the calves like I told you. But no, you had to send 'em on down the coast with the other men and you and me ride this trail you heard Matt talk so much about."

El Gato touched his hip. "That'll be all from you, Jake."

The man subsided. Meekly, he dismounted and tied his pony.

"Where's Matt?" El Gato asked.

"Behind me," Jake answered sullenly.

"How'd he get there? I told you to keep your eyes on him if you meant to keep healthy. He'd better show up pronto."

Slowly the third man rode in.

As he passed into closer view, Robin gasped and clutched Mindy's arm. "Look at the man they call Matt," she whispered. "Do you know who he is?"

"The man we saw on Roberto Street!" Mindy exclaimed. "That little boy's father. I guess he found work all right. Terrible work. Did you hear what that man said about trucks—and 'critters'? They've been stealing cattle from Rancho Lucia!"

"Then they have Nugget!" Robin groaned under her breath. "Oh, Mindy! That little boy's father helped steal Nugget. What *shall* we do now?"

"Keep under cover and not make a sound. That's what we'll do if we want to save our lives. Thank heaven the ponies are down the mesa out of sight. Those men would kill us the minute they saw us. Crouch down, Robin . . . low . . . out of sight. . . . Oh, do be careful!"

Robin groaned. "What have they done to Nugget? It's all I can do to keep from asking them."

"Don't you *dare* say a word to them! Don't you

dare let them know we're here. Oh, please be still, Robin. They'd drop us over the canyon edge. Nobody would ever know what happened to us. We'd never see our families again. Just this once, Robin, do be quiet and careful!"

5. *In the Cave*

EL GATO SWUNG around suddenly to face the cave where the girls crouched, hidden. Robin's heart turned cold. Her veins were icicles. Had he heard their voices?

"We could have gone in that cave if we'd been here in time," El Gato snarled. "I hate rain."

"Yeah, all cats do," Jake said, then cringed at El Gato's contemptuous laugh.

"I might take a look in there just in case we come this way again. It'd make a good overnight stop. Stream close by. Looks like it might be cozy."

Inside, the girls stopped breathing. "Move over farther," Mindy urged desperately. "Can you?"

"No, but I can pray. I'm doing it. You pray, too."

Mindy put her head down, pressed close to Robin. "That terrible man can't possibly come in here!"

"I . . . think . . . he's . . . going to. Oh, Mindy, it's all over!"

Through their terror, Jake's voice came to them. "Go into the cave if you want to, El Gato. It's your funeral. I mean it. Where do you suppose wildcats go when it rains—huh?"

El Gato bounded away from the opening so fast that he sprawled in the mud. Jake slapped his knees and roared. "Not that I'd miss you if a wildcat mauled you. I'd only miss the loot we'll have when we finish this job. Let's get goin'. How d'ya ever expect to get underway with the calves if we stop at every wide place on the trail? The gang at the load-in' place is sweatin' now you can bet, wonderin' what's holdin' us up. You and Matt and that horse! Cost us a good half day."

The dark man spat almost in Jake's face. "El Gato is the leader of this outfit," he said sternly. "He says where to stop and when to move on. They'll see us when we get there, and it will be before dark, my friend."

Watching, listening, Robin gasped. "A horse! Mindy, did you hear that? It's Nugget. Listen! What's Matt saying?"

"I wish I'd never talked about this ranch country. If I hadn't you'd never have come here. I don't want any part in what you're mixed up in," Matt told El Gato and Jake, his face very serious. "I've kept telling you that. You can't count on me for anything crooked. Rustlin' cattle can mean life and I've had all I can take."

"Oh, you have, have you?" El Gato sneered. "You didn't feel so pious back in the Yard at the Big House when we planned to do this job as soon as we were sprung."

"I told you then that I wouldn't be in on anything crooked," Matt insisted. "You know that with my wife gone I've got a kid to support. I'm all he has. I don't want him to be ashamed of me."

El Gato swaggered over to Matt, put his evil face close and said, "That's a laugh. No kid is ever goin' to be proud of a jailbird father. Take the game that goes with the name, big boy. Go get some dough to help take care of the kid. Dough talks. Not tears. Who's goin' to give a jailbird a legitimate job?"

The girls, cramped in the small pocket in the cave, listened for Matt's answer. Robin waited for just one thing—news of Nugget.

"That's the tough part. I never should have been put in that pen. I was framed. I never had a chance."

"You've got your chance now, big boy," El Gato said.

"Yeah," Jake added.

"You're in with us, like it or not," El Gato went on. "We have to have another hand to load the calves down on the coast. Boats don't wait for anyone. Take your choice. Help us or . . . go over the side of the canyon feet first and tied!"

El Gato leveled his gun at Matt. "That was a pretty thin story you told us, too, about last night, big boy. About that horse breakin' loose while me and Jake was asleep. And about your kid disappearin'. You think someone's goin' to find him and look after him? I'm pretty sure they will, because I think I know how you took care of the kid and the horse. Did you think we didn't know a horse like that would bring a thousand dollars anywhere between here and the border? Even if you told the truth, you shouldn't of let the horse and kid get away. We owe you somethin' for that."

"Sure I took care of Jeff. He's safe from you and everyone else. The kind of chance I'm talking about isn't the kind you have to offer. I'm not going to do any dirty work for anyone. I'm going to think of my kid."

El Gato laughed wickedly. "A lot of good you'll do him down there in the canyon with the buzzards circlin' over you. Just keep your mouth shut and play along with me. There's plenty more calves where the ones we got came from. We've gotta make time before the ranch starts brandin' 'em. No brand, no proof. See?" El Gato poked his gun into Matt's ribs. "Get goin'!"

With an oath, he walked over to his black pony, adjusted the saddle impatiently, and tightened the girth. Then he slapped his hand reassuringly on the bulge in his hip pocket and, with a sneer of contempt toward Matt, motioned him to mount and ride on ahead.

Back in their refuge the girls waited, tense and

miserable, until they heard the thud of the ponies' hoofs far along the trail. Then slowly, like frightened mice, they came out.

"That's the man I have to follow," Robin said. "Matt, the boy's father. He's the one who knows where Nugget is."

"For heaven's sake, Robin, you can't do that now! He's with El Gato. Didn't you see the gun? Look where the sun is in the sky. We'll be lucky if we get down the trail before dark. Even in broad daylight it isn't too easy to follow."

"But Nugget!" Robin persisted. "Mindy, I just have to find him."

"There's one thing sure: Nugget isn't with those men. Where did you get the idea that he is? Didn't you hear what El Gato said about the horse getting away from Matt? The thing for us to do is to ride back to the ranch, tell them all we know as soon as we can, and let Sheriff Jackson take over from there."

"Do you honestly think that's the best thing to do? I'm so worried I can't think straight. I know Nugget *had* been with them. I'm sure Matt knows where he is now."

"Yes, I think he does. If he does, it's still the best

thing to do—to leave it to the sheriff. Please go with me now, Robin. I want to put as much distance between us and El Gato as possible. I should think you'd feel the same way. I never was so scared in all my life."

Bueno and Sugar stood placidly at the edge of the swollen stream, cropping grass. So far as they were concerned there might never have been a storm. Mindy took two apples from the bag in which they had packed sandwiches. She gave one to Robin and held the other in her flattened palm for Sugar.

"Give that one to Bueno," she told Robin. "Haven't they been good?" She stroked Sugar's long neck. "If they'd made one sound when El Gato was here it would have been fatal."

Bueno crunched his apple while Robin put her arm around his thin brown neck and leaned close. "They've been wonderful!" Then her eyes clouded. "We haven't accomplished one thing. Nugget is still missing. If Matt has him, what did he do with him? What did he do with his little boy?"

"The whole thing is a mystery. We are certain of one thing: Matt loves little Jeff. He'd take care of him. I think he loves horses, too. He petted that pony he had to ride. Try to imagine Nugget will be all right till we get him back. There's one thing you forget: My daddy's calves were stolen, too. We know positively who stole them. That's something accomplished."

Quickly penitent, Robin said, "Oh, I did forget that. I have a one-track mind."

"Never mind. I should honestly think, though, that you'd trust Nugget with Matt quicker than you would with El Gato."

"A thousand times quicker. It was all I could do to keep from walking right out of that cave and loosening that bit on El Gato's pony. He's a wicked, cruel man."

"He sure is. We've had a narrow escape. Let's hurry and get on the trail!"

Bueno and Sugar seemed glad to go, too. The rain had turned the hard clay trail into slimy mud, though, and the going was rough. Robin rode ahead coaxing Bueno, reaching to pat him encouragingly now and then. "There, there, pick up your feet, Bueno! Stay away from that awful edge!"

"This is the worst part of the whole trail," Mindy

called. "I keep remembering what El Gato said to Matt about the buzzards."

Robin reined in Bueno, slipped from the saddle. "Don't think of it, Mindy. Don't dare think of it! If we hug the hillside real close we'll make it all right. We'd better lead the ponies for a while. Gosh, these tennis shoes are so soaked, they'd slip on sandpaper. There, Bueno. . . . Good boy! Careful!"

Slowly, never daring to look to the canyon side of the trail, Robin and Mindy picked their way along.

Once, close behind her, Mindy's pony slipped, recovered himself.

"Good boy, Sugar!" Mindy murmured. "That was a close one. It can't be long now till the trail leaves this edge of the canyon. Maybe it'd be better just to drop the reins. . . ."

"Let's do that!" Robin said quickly. "The ponies can follow us. They know the trail better than we do."

"It's the rain that has made all the trouble. That adobe mud is like glue. The other side of the mountain where those men are going is even worse. Their trail skirts the canyon all the way down. Robin—I just happened to think of something."

"I wonder if it's what I'm thinking. If those calves were already being loaded on the trucks, why did they need Matt? I'm afraid they may have—"

"Done away with him? That's exactly what I thought. Oh, we just have to hurry and get word to Sheriff Jackson."

Robin shuddered. "He can't send a posse into the woods tonight. That means they'll have almost a day's start from the mesa . . . those men."

"The sheriff will alert all the sheriffs in the towns below here. You forgot about that."

"Suppose Matt won't go any farther with them. Suppose they don't even intend to take him—that they mean to murder him because of what he already knows." Robin's voice broke. "Then who will take care of little Jeff? We *have* to hurry, Mindy. Oh, can't you hurry any faster? Will this awful slippery trail never end?"

"Don't let your imagination run away with you, Robin. Don't you think if El Gato and Jake had been going to do away with Matt they'd have shot him as soon as they found out he'd taken Jeff and Nugget someplace else?"

"Oh, dear! Yes, right in front of our very eyes, maybe. It's terrible, Mindy. I'm just beginning to realize—"

"What a narrow escape we've had. I know. I can't bear to think about it. Say, Robin, look down there below us."

"All those lights bobbing in the dusk. Can it be the Rancho?"

"It is! We're almost there! Those are the lanterns the cowboys carry to do their milking. Oh, Robin, I do love our dear families!"

In the flat field at the foot of the slope a crowd of riders rode to meet the girls. Mr. Hunter and Mr. Kane led the way, then Michael and Kevin, Moira and half a dozen cowboys.

They formed a ring around the girls. "Are you all right?" Mr. Hunter asked anxiously. "You both look as though you'd seen a ghost."

"We've seen worse than that," Robin said wearily. "Wait till we get to the house and then you just listen to what we have to tell you." She turned to her father. "Oh, Daddy, I'm so glad to see you. How did you happen to be here?"

"Your mother and Amy and I just arrived. Mr.

Hunter sent for us when you girls were so late in getting back. Robin, honey, what happened?"

"I'll tell you. Right away." Robin pressed Bueno's sides, and he trotted along briskly.

At the ranch house everyone started talking at once.

"That's enough," Mr. Hunter said. "Something has upset the girls badly. When they've rested a little we'll find out what it was. Don't cry, Mrs. Kane. They're back safely, thank God!"

"We can't wait, Mr. Hunter. I'm sorry," Robin said. "We've just got to tell you what happened right now. Sheriff Jackson has to know."

"All right. Sit down here now. Let's hear it."

"But, Mr. Hunter," Amy interrupted, "Robin and Mindy don't even know—"

"We don't know what?" Robin asked eagerly. "Has Nugget been found? Is there news of him?"

Mr. Hunter shook his head. "No. I'm sorry."

"It's Rancho Lucia's calves!" Amy shouted. "Someone stole about fifty of those darling little white-faced calves!"

"We *know* that," Robin and Mindy said in a single voice.

"You do?" Amy asked. Everyone gasped.

"Yes, Sugar," Mindy answered. "It's what we were going to tell you, Daddy. Oh, Moira, I'm glad you weren't with us. It was ghastly. Daddy—listen—"

"We know who stole them!" Robin jumped from her chair dramatically. "We saw the men, Mr. Hunter. They almost stole us, too. You tell it, Mindy."

Mrs. Kane, who sat at Robin's side, gripped her daughter's hand hard as the story unfolded. Mr. Kane and Mr. Hunter sat white-faced and silent.

At the close of the story, Mr. Hunter went to the telephone in the corner of the room and dialed Sheriff Jackson's number.

"We know who has the calves," he said. "We have a good idea of where you must look for them. . . . Yes. El Gato and his outfit, just as you thought. . . . Come over to the ranch and I'll tell you what happened. It's been pretty rugged. My daughter and Robin Kane ran into the thieves on the edge of the canyon —Mesa Aguidera. . . . No, they were hiding in the cave there, from the rain. I'll ask them to tell you what they saw and heard when you get here."

On the screened patio Mamacita loaded the table with all the good food the ranch provided.

Darkness came.

Through the screen, crickets could be heard tuning up, and doves cooing softly. Rose geraniums and night-blooming jasmine sent their fragrance to mingle with the tart aroma of *tacos, enchiladas* and hot peppered beans. No one had eaten yet. They had all been too worried about Robin and Mindy.

Now, everybody began to talk at once. Questions were hurled at the girls and they answered till their voices broke with exhaustion.

"I just can't remember another thing," Mindy finally said as she left the table. "Let's go home with Michael, Moira. We can all get together tomorrow. Daddy and Mr. Rafferty can talk to the sheriff when he comes . . . your dad, too, Robin. You come with us."

"No. I'm not a bit tired. Do you think I can sleep a wink till Sheriff Jackson finds out something about Nugget?"

Patiently Mr. Hunter tried to explain. "You've just traveled that muddy, slippery trail in daylight. Do you think anyone could get over it at night?"

"I guess not, but think of what may be happening to Matt. It makes me sick to think the sheriff and his men may not be able to catch up with El Gato at all if he gets a whole night's start."

"Right now the sheriff is getting in touch with other sheriffs down the coast telling them what we know," Mr. Hunter said. "It's pretty certain that El Gato and his men are beyond the mountain by now. We can't help Matt any by losing men and ponies searching at night. I wish you could have learned more about where El Gato was headed for."

"Over the border, I think. He and Jake talked so fast and swore so much I didn't hear everything they said. I'm sorry."

"Well, cheer up, honey," Mr. Hunter said quietly. "Fifty or more lively, bawling calves will be pretty hard to keep under cover. The sheriff's office will have news for us in the morning. Just wait and see."

6. *Water-Skiing*

IN SPITE OF Mr. Hunter's optimism, there wasn't any news of Nugget or the missing calves the next morning, not even by ten o'clock when Robin and her mother were doing the breakfast dishes. Robin was sad and discouraged. "If Mindy had only gone on with me after we saw those men, we might have found out where they were going. We could have followed Matt and we'd have found Nugget."

"Probably no one would ever have found you or Mindy again," her mother said soberly. "Just don't mention that possibility to me. You worry me a great deal with all the chances you take. Leave the matter to Sheriff Jackson, as Mindy's father said. You'll see that it will turn out all right. Two girls alone on that wilderness hillside! I just can't bear to think of what might have happened. I hope you'll never take a chance like that again."

"Oh, Mother, you don't understand. It's Nugget. Nobody seems to understand."

"I understand that someone's been honking a horn at the patio gate. See who it is, please."

A laughing, shouting group thronged into the kitchen. Mindy came first. "Guess what! The best news! Moira's going to have two, maybe three days' vacation, and she's going to spend it here at Pacific Point."

"I begged for it," Moira said. "Mr. Hunter told me they'd shoot the picture around me down at the Hearst Castle, San Simeon. I don't have to be in any of the scenes there. Not one of the principals has to be there. They'll just be shooting scenery for background. I'm so excited! I haven't even had one day off for months. I'd rather be right here, too, than any place I know except my very own home. My daddo's at Rancho Lucia. He loves to be there with the cows and horses. He loves the outdoors."

Immediately Robin's face turned from despair to delight as the Irish girl grasped her hands and danced her around the room.

"Oh, I hope you're as happy as I am, Robin," said Moira.

"It's super!" Robin's mind began to plan. "Just two days? It has to be three, at least. Let me see." She looked around at the excited faces. "We'll have a beach party today."

"Water-skiing first," Michael interrupted. "Moira has never been on skis in her life."

"And I'm that scared I'd die dead!"

"Not with Michael teaching you," Amy spoke up. "He taught me. I think he's taught everybody, Moira."

"Has he, Sugar? Once in Santa Barbara I was supposed to water-ski in a part I had. I didn't tell anyone I couldn't do it. I wanted the part so! I thought all a person had to do was to stand on those skis and skip along back of a boat. Ohhh, what a bad time I had of it! I'd love to learn now. I may be asked to do it again. Will it take long? I can swim very well."

"Judy learned in half an hour. If she could—well, Judy's my best friend," Amy said. "Michael, can—*may* she go with us today?"

"Sure enough, Sugar. We'll pick her up on our way. Moira, it'll be a breeze for you to learn to ski. Kevin, I can have the inboard boat today. You'll drive it, won't you?"

"Yeah. You'll be the big shot on skis. Moira, do you ever have to ride a surfboard in any of your pictures?"

"I did. A little. Glory, but it's hard to do."

"Not for Kevin," Mindy sang out. "He's the champion surfboarder of the peninsula."

"A lot of good that'll do me now. It takes time to learn surfing safely. You'd have to stay all summer." Kevin's face lighted up. "Say, why couldn't you do that?"

Moira clapped her hands, laughed out loud. "Imagine you all wanting me to! It's not that I'd not like to do it. Picture making is hard, hard work. But today— Say, let's get going, as you say in this country."

"Mom, is it all right? We'll be gone all day. That is, we'll be gone all morning, at least. Then again in the afternoon and evening."

"It's all right so far as your home chores are concerned, Robin. I suppose you've arranged with Mrs. Norville to be free today. This *is* the day you shelve books for her in the children's library, isn't it?"

"Oh, that!" Robin answered briskly. "I don't think it will make any difference to Mrs. Norville. It isn't as though Mindy and I were paid for doing the work."

"What are you saying? You've always been so proud of that work. A job a person volunteers to do carries an obligation even greater than a paid job."

Robin's face reddened. "You're right, Mom. I forgot. I guess I've been so upset I didn't think straight. We do get paid, too, Mindy and I, when we see the fun the little kids have with the books. I'll go right away, if Michael will wait for me. I'll see if Mrs. Norville will excuse me for the day."

"Don't worry," Michael said quickly. "Mindy and I stopped at the library. Mrs. Norville said she wouldn't need either one of you today. The recreation director gave Kevin and me time off, too, from running the rake on the beach. Now don't let your conscience bother you."

"I'm afraid I wasn't letting it bother me enough. That's always my trouble. I'm glad, though, Michael, and thanks for clearing the way for Kevin and me. It's all right now, isn't it, Mom?"

"Of course. Come back here after you ski and I'll have something for you all to eat."

"Not today," Mindy said. "Thanks a million, Mrs. Kane, but today Daddy said for us to go to the Beach and Tennis Club. We'll be right there on Clearwater Cove anyway. Something else, too. Tomorrow morning Manuela wants to get a Spanish breakfast for us at our house."

"I'll really have a family of Fatsos with all that eating," Mrs. Kane said, smiling. "I'd like to have some part in the fun of having Moira here. How about tonight? Are you going to have a beach picnic? Then I'll fix hampers for that. When you leave the club stop by here for your surfboards and the picnic hampers. There may be a surprise in them."

"My mom always has surprises," Amy said. "Let's go out to the Huddle and get our skis."

"Do you all have swimsuits on under those jeans and shorts?"

"Yep," Kevin said. "I'm always dressed for a swim."

"Every one of you does the same thing. Moira, is yours a family of water rats, too?"

"Yes, ma'am, but the shore around Glenbeigh where I live is rocky and rough. No beach there at all. We swim in pools after high tide and hunt for mussels when the moon comes up over Dingle Bay. There's no water-skiing. No surfing."

"Come on!" Amy said, tugging at Moira's arm. "As Daddy always says, 'Time's running out.' "

Tramp followed them to the gate and stood there begging with big brown eyes and little whines.

"Can he come, Michael?" Amy asked.

"Not this morning, Sugar, but tell him he may go to the beach with us this afternoon. Is that all right, fella?"

Tramp didn't think so, and said so with sharp barks.

The station wagon disappeared down the beach road, pointed water skis bristling at all side and back windows.

"First we have to pick up Judy, you know," Amy said.

"That's just where I'm going, Sugar." Michael drove up the hill from the shore. "She's ready, too.

See her there with her skis?"

"I'll get out and carry them for her," Kevin said, but Robin put out her hand to stop him. "Don't Kev. She's so independent."

A small, tanned girl with pigtails flying ran haltingly out to the car as it stopped. Moira, her face registering instant realization, gasped in pity.

"Polio," Robin whispered. "Don't pay any attention. Judy never does."

Kevin took the girl's skis and added them to the pile in the wagon. "This is Moira Rafferty," he told Judy.

The little girl turned her rapturous face to Moira and said shyly, "I know."

"She's afraid of skis, honey," Michael said. "She's never been on them. You should see Judy on skis, Moira. But then you will. She's a whiz."

"Michael taught me. He'll teach you, Moira, and you'll never be afraid again. I'm a member of your fan club," she added softly.

"Well, I'll bet you I'll be a member of *your* fan club when I see you ski," Moira said, and made room for Judy next to her.

The boat was moored at the cove near the Club.

It was stripped for greatest ease in racing through the water drawing tow ropes. Open, too, from front to stern, the freeboard was low for easy boarding from the water.

"I suppose you want to teach Moira the basic steps in skiing, don't you, Mike?" Kevin asked.

"Sure. I'll start her off over there on the sand, and then in shallow water. Why?"

"I thought I'd take the kids for a spin around the cove on skis till you think Moira's ready to follow the boat."

At his words Judy and Amy pulled their skis from the wagon and started for deep water.

Back on the sand Moira said determinedly, "If that little girl can ski, I can. What do I do first, Michael?"

"You take your skis out of the wagon," Robin said, laughing. "Here they are. I'll go with Judy and Sugar. Coming, Mindy?"

"No, I'll stay here and watch Moira."

"To stiffen my back," Moira smiled.

"Mike will tell you that's the last way in the world to stand on skis," Robin called. "We'll see you later."

She took her own skis and waded out into the

water where the little girls were waiting in position for the boat to pull them up.

"Don't try any of your stunts today, Judy!" she warned. "You can't cut across the wake of the boat when three of us are being towed."

"I know that," Judy said and her chin went up. "One thing Michael told me never to do was to show off, and I don't. He said you only land in the water."

"Upside down, too. Don't forget that. Ready, girls?"

They nodded vigorously.

"Then hit it!" Robin called to Kevin. He started the boat slowly, as all good ski drivers do, and pulled the three girls and their towlines gracefully out of the water.

As he accelerated the motor and picked up speed, the girls sailed over the water like flying fish. Judy's pigtails stood straight out behind her. Her face was ecstatic. White water broke back of the tow ropes as Kevin drew them in a wide arc to skirt the cove's shoreline.

Once, when they passed Michael and Moira and Mindy, the Irish girl was standing on her skis, with Michael pulling at the tow rope. Judy and Amy cheered as they skied past. At the sound Moira went splashing into the shallows.

"Let's keep away from her," Robin told Kev when the boat stopped. "She'll do better if she isn't watched. It won't be long now till Michael will signal us to let her try it in back of the boat."

It wasn't long.

It took only four or five tries till Moira, a bit wobbly, but determined, was sailing along side by side with Mike. The little girls, in the boat with Kevin and Robin, cheered her on, laughing delightedly at her rapturous face as she skimmed the water.

Later, after the girls had toweled their hair dry and wrapped skirts around their swimsuits, they joined the blue-jeaned boys for lunch in the big dining room of the Club.

If Moira had been unrecognized on the beach, she lost her anonymity in the dining room. Young people crowded around for her autograph. Although she gave it willingly with a gracious word and smile, her face showed how much she longed to be just like Robin and Mindy. If she felt that way, Amy and Judy didn't. They glowed with reflected glory. Their idol was there, and all the youngsters in the room knew it. It was keeno, as Amy said afterward.

After the delicious luncheon of shrimp and piping hot rolls, they walked out on the big veranda where the white-capped waves crept to the very steps.

Moira had brought a small camera. In a few shots she recorded the beauty that was all around: blue sky, rolling waves, low dark cypresses pushing their shadows toward the lapping water. When Amy and Judy asked for it, she turned her camera over to Robin and posed with the girls.

"I'll send you prints," she promised.

The veranda was filled with people watching. Robin, sensing Moira's dismay, called to Michael, "Time now to go back to the house for the picnic hampers, isn't it?"

"Time now for Mike to take to the background," Kevin answered, laughing. "I can't teach Moira to surf in a day, but once down on the Point I can show her what she's missing."

"Could anyone in the world be having more fun than I, myself?" Moira asked as they rounded the clubhouse drive and turned toward Pacific Point.

"It's not over yet," Amy told her and squeezed

Moira's hand. "Don't think it isn't fun for us. Why, what's the matter, Judy?"

Judy's small brown face was squeezed into seriousness. "Nothing. Why?"

"Well, gosh, we've had so much fun and here you are looking absolutely droopy. Why?"

"I guess it's because it's all over—for me," Judy said in a whisper.

"What do you mean 'all over'?" Amy asked. "We're going to the beach, aren't we? Kev and Michael will ride the surf. You and I will look for driftwood for Mom's little figures she makes. Then we'll all have supper there and a fire . . . just everything. What's the matter with you?"

"You mean I'm invited for all that?" Judy asked, her eyes big and round.

"Of course! Didn't you know it wouldn't be any fun at all without you?" Robin asked. She put her arm around the little girl and drew her close. "I'll whisper something to you, if the rest will forgive me. It's this, honey bug: Moira never in all the world would have learned to water-ski if she hadn't watched how good you are at it."

"Honest?" Judy asked.

"Cross my heart. Will we have to stop at your house and tell your mom you'll be with us till way after dark?"

"I guess not. I sort of hoped. She'll know where I am. Oh, Robin!"

7. *The Same Pelican*

BACK AT the Kane home they all talked at once, trying to describe their morning to Robin's mother and father.

Careful not to attract attention, Robin drew her mother aside. "Has there been any word at all from Rancho Lucia about Nugget?"

"Not about Nugget, but an odd thing seems to have happened about El Gato and the other two men."

"What is it, Mom?"

"Sheriff Jackson traced them down the coast as

far as Breakwater. Then they disappeared."

"They couldn't!"

"They did. The men stopped at a restaurant at Breakwater, and Nick, the man who runs it, saw the trucks. From then on—nothing!"

"Had anyone seen a palomino? Mom, had they?"

"No, Robin. I asked. No one anywhere had seen a palomino."

"There goes my last hope."

"Not at all. The sheriff is on the trail of El Gato. Aside from that, he's making an independent search for Nugget. He said a lost boy would have been found, and if Nugget had been turned loose he'd have found his way back to the ranch; that man or boy or both would have followed the established trail. He's sure that when you heard Matt say he'd taken care of the boy, he meant he had taken him to some hideaway in the woods. He thinks Nugget may be there, too, and believes it will take a miracle to discover where."

"Then there'll have to be a miracle."

"I'm terribly sorry, Robin, that it is all going so slowly. I know how you feel. I'm proud of you for not showing it in front of Moira. It would spoil her vacation." She smiled at Robin fondly.

"No matter how I try to hide it, Mom, Mindy and Moira both know how worried I am. I must go back now where the others are. Oh, how I do hope and pray for some word from my wonderful horse."

When she went out to the patio, Mindy said, "Your dad just told us there's no good word about Nugget and the calves, Robin. They just couldn't have vanished as the sheriff said. Not all those calves, trucks, and men."

"And Nugget," Robin said in a hopeless tone. Then, summoning all her courage, she said brightly, "Maybe we'll have better word tomorrow. Mom, are the hampers ready? Daddy, don't you dare put Moira in one of your comic strips! He will, Moira, and he'll have you saying 'begorra' and maybe smoking a clay pipe."

"Sure and begorra, you'd better not!" Moira said, laughing. "I never in my life heard a man in Ireland say 'begorra.' "

"I'll make a leprechaun out of you in my strip," Mr. Kane promised. "You're like a little leprechaun in *The Changeling*—first one kind of girl, then another. Would you like that?"

"So long as I'd be one of the little people I'd not mind at all what you'd do with me in your strip. Did you know that it runs in a Dublin paper?"

"No, I didn't, but I'm glad. My ancestors came from Ireland, Moira. From almost next door to you, in County Clare. We were there last summer, my wife and I."

"Oh, my, is that true?" Moira looked around her. "Then it means you'll all be coming over to visit again, maybe next summer? It's but a skip and a jump from Glenbeigh to the Clare border. Now I feel even more at home."

"Come in here and see some of Mom's little driftwood figures," Amy called from the next room. "I don't know what leprechauns look like but they *sound* like Mom's figures look. This one," she held a five-inch figure in her hand, "could be an Irish gnome. He isn't, though, in spite of his beard. He's Moses. He looked just like this when Mom found him. She mounted him, though, and smoothed him down a little. See this mermaid with long blond hair? And here are two little girls. Mom calls them Amy and Judy."

"They're darling!" Moira crouched down to look at the dainty bits of driftwood on the cabinet shelves.

"We used to laugh at Mom 'cause she was always picking up driftwood whenever we went to the beach," Kevin said.

"We don't any more!" Robin said definitely. "Not after Drummond's in San Francisco sells every one she'll send them. For fat prices, too."

Mrs. Kane smiled modestly. "Isn't it fantastic? They just looked like people to me and I brought them home and mounted them on small pedestals. It's fun. Let's have no more about me, though. The hampers are packed. The vacuum chest is full of Cokes. Have fun!"

"How about coming with us?" Mindy asked. "You and Mr. Kane."

"Yeah, Mom," Kevin urged and added to Moira, "Mom bends a mean knee on water skis herself."

"I don't exactly have a gray beard clear down to here, Kevin," Mrs. Kane said and held her palm to her waist.

"You're an exactly right kind of mom," Mindy said, hugging her. "I'm glad you've sort of adopted Michael and me. We'd love to have you both come with us. Do you think you can?"

"We'd like it, too," Mr. Kane answered. "But we have an engagement to play bridge with the Gardners in Lobos Heights. Moira, don't let them drown you. Watch out for Judy and Amy, all of you!"

"Dad!" Amy said, disgusted. "I'm going on eleven years old!"

"One month past ten," Kevin said, laughing. "Come on, Sugar. You can help me get the surfboards."

When they crowded into the car there sat Tramp, tongue out, thumping his tail as much as to say, "Here I am. You promised, you know."

"Good dog!" Michael said. "Crowd over a little, give me room to drive or—better yet—get in the back with Sugar."

Down at the Point, Michael wheeled in and parked with a swish of sand.

"Surf's up!" a wave watcher called, recognizing Kevin. Then Kevin and Michael, so excited they forgot all about the girls, grabbed their boards, shed blue jeans that covered their swimming trunks, and ran toward the foam.

Lying prone on their boards, they paddled like great turtles out through the surf.

Mindy, Moira, Amy, and Judy lined up on the shore to watch. Tramp watched, too, barking happily at nothing.

Beautiful lines were breaking beyond a rock formation well out in the ocean. Near shore, surfers were picking up medium waves and getting good rides.

A set of big ones came through, their dark green tips frosted with foam blown by an offshore wind, their glassy left sides holding beautifully.

"Cowabunga!" Judy called, dancing on one foot, frantically waving at the glistening blue and red boards that bore Kevin and Michael.

"It doesn't look too hard to do," Moira said. "I only tried the littlest kind of swell at Santa Barbara. Just look at the way those surfers are riding—standing up! Where are the boys?"

"Oh, they're doing it the hard way," Robin said. "Over there back of the rocks waiting for the 'ninth wave.' Everyone else is content to pick up the waves this side of the rock. Not Kevin and Michael. I wish Michael wouldn't take chances. Kevin's all right, but

Michael can't ride a board the way he can."

"Oh, Mike's fine," Mindy said. "You worry when he's out in the surf, and he worries about all the chances you take."

"Michael's a skier," Robin said seriously to Moira, "and a good one. It's a lot different. When you ski you hold on to a tow rope. Out there if you start to tip you reach for a sky hook and nothing's there. Ohhhhh! I knew it would happen! Did you see them? Do you see Michael? Kevin's all right. I see his board."

"So's Michael," Judy said. "Boy, did you see the way he soared over the top of that wave?"

"I saw him crouch to get ready," Robin said.

"Then he wiped out!" Amy called. "There he comes now, washed up on the shore break, right there on the beach. See him, Robin? See his red board?"

"This isn't my day," Michael said, a grin across his freckled face. "It isn't my sport, either. Watch Kev!"

Out beyond the rocks, Kevin paddled and idled, waiting for that magic ninth. When it came in, hollow and curling, he caught it with one stroke.

His bright blue board glistened in the mid-afternoon sun as he went up to the crest and came angling down under, almost touching the rocks. One mistake and his board would have shattered.

On shore, the little beach bunnies, Amy and Judy, watched breathlessly. Robin wasn't worried. She knew what Kevin could do. So did Mindy.

"Gol!" Michael said in admiration as Kevin, with a shout of sheer jubilation turned, pulled out, and —riding easily and jauntily—beached his board.

A shout went up, too, from the watchers on shore. Kevin, peninsula champion, was their idol. He took the applause, hand on heart, clowning and loving every minute of it.

"Part of it may be clowning," Robin thought to herself, "but Kevin's super. He knows, and I do, and so do Mike and Mindy, that it's a real skill to have whipped through a greedy licking like that wave and come in standing."

Urged on by the boys, the girls, big and little, took their boards into the low, coast-hugging surf. There was plenty of fun there and little danger, splashing, wiping out, trying again.

On shore, when Kevin and Michael had dried

themselves in the sun, they hunted big chunks of driftwood for a fire. One by one, the girls straggled to shore to help.

The afternoon sun was low in the sky. The ocean, empty now of surfers or bathers (for regulations were rigid), rippled in the waning light. Most of the crowd had disappeared. On the horizon, a haze crept nearer and nearer inshore as fog shrouded the water and sent its long tongues winding in and around the gnarled cypresses.

Here and there at intervals fires blazed, then dimmed as wood caught and glowed for waiting hamburgers or weiners.

Mindy and Moira opened the hampers the boys brought from the wagon. Judy and Amy watched, eyes big and hopeful.

With sharpened sticks, they all roasted hot dogs and then put them on buttered buns and topped them with mustard and pickles. There were deviled eggs, Amy's favorite food, a crisp salad and, to top the feast, Mrs. Kane's "surprise." Amy brought it, wax-paper covered, a luscious chocolate cake rich with foamy frosting.

The wind freshened and a silver moon crept up

the sky through the haze. Down the shore somewhere a guitar could be heard.

"You did bring your guitar, didn't you, Kevin?" Judy asked wistfully. She and Amy sat near the dying fire, Tramp's head blissfully and sleepily in Amy's lap.

"I sure did, honey. Here it is. Listen to that backbeat down the shore, Robin. It sounds just like the Surf Boys. Hold on a minute. I'll see if I can catch it. There! Everybody sing!

"I'm paddlin' through the surf and lookin'
for the ninth wave.
Waitin'. Watchin'. Waitin'.
There's an offshore wind and a heavy swell
comin' past the beach.
There's an offshore wind and a heavy swell
comin' past the beach.
I'm waitin'. Yes, I'm waitin'. I'm waitin'.
Late at night when the crowd's not here
and I'm all alone and the moon shines clear,
I'm waitin'. Waitin'. Waitin'.
For the big ninth wave to come rollin' in.
Just waitin'. Watchin'. Waitin'."

"Play it again!" the girls begged.

Kevin did, and everyone clapped and sang in the beat of the waves, the wash of the surf, and the lapping echo of ripples running up the sand.

When he stopped, Kevin handed his guitar to Moira.

"I heard you snap some real chords in that movie, *Roll, Pacific,"* he said. "Sing something, please. Something Irish, Moira."

Moira took the guitar with a smile, strummed a few chords, and then began in a clear, sweet voice:

"There's a low voice callin' to me from
the sea,
A lonely voice callin', whisht! Listen, all
ye.
'Tis the words of my Johnny asayin' to me—
Listen! Whisht, listen!
Do you hear what he's tellin'?
Repeatin' my name?
My Johnny was drowned in cruel Bantry
Bay,
In a sea that was cruel, and cruel was
the day.

But whisht! If you'll listen, you'll hear him
so plain
Sayin', 'Mary, I love you,' again and again,
Sayin', 'Mary, I love you,' again and again,
Sayin', 'Mary, I love you,' again and again."

Judy sighed blissfully, drowsily. "It's been such a beautiful day. It shouldn't ever, ever end."

"You took the words right out of my heart," Moira agreed, stretching her slender arms above her. "Robin, what are those lights? Out there, rounding the Point, green light, then white?"

Kevin and Michael were on their feet instantly. Tramp, startled out of Amy's lap, jumped up, barking.

"They're running lights," Michael said. "Some kind of craft. It's running pretty close to shore if it's a sailboat. Plenty of wind, though. Boy, whoever's sailing it knows how to handle the tiller."

"It's odd to see a sailboat this far from still water, isn't it, Michael?" Robin asked.

"Yeah. A little more than odd."

They lined up, straining their eyes to identify the shape that crept nearer in the mist. All at once, when the dark bulk was directly in front of them, the fog parted, and the moon shone bright just for a moment. In that moment Robin gasped, stifled a low moan.

"Did you see it?" she whispered hoarsely. "The pelican? That flying bird on the spinnaker?"

"She had 'The Ancient Mariner' in English last year," Kevin said, laughing. "She thinks now that she saw the albatross."

"I don't think so, Kev," Michael answered, his kindly freckled face serious. "Remember the blue pelican on the corral fence? Put there when Nugget disappeared?"

Robin's voice rose. "The very same drawing was on that sail. The same pelican. A blue one—in flight. Oh, why does it have to be so foggy? I couldn't see who was at the tiller, but it's Matt on that boat! I know it is. We have to catch up and see where he stops. Just gather the rest of the cake in the tablecloth, Sugar. Let's run. Mike, hurry and start the motor. That man knows where Nugget is."

In the space of two minutes the car was on its way. It roared up Ocean Avenue and stopped with screaming brakes at the police station. Then, with the police chief in the front seat with Michael and Kevin it sped to the beach road.

At the foot of Ocean Avenue the young people fixed their eyes on the fog-bound shore, breathlessly waiting. The boat couldn't have passed in the short time they were picking up the chief. There was no place for it to go except inshore. Way out in the ocean big waves were breaking.

Suddenly Robin gasped. What was that creeping along, dimmed in the haze?

"It's the boat!" Robin shouted. "I see its running lights, see? Green on the port side. White tip on the main mast. Doesn't *anyone* else see them? I can't be imagining them."

"I see the boat, Robin," Judy said. Her sharp little eyes found it sailing well within the quiet water and at full sail.

"We'll follow this road slowly," the chief told Michael. "The boat's bound to wind up at Clearwater Cove. Whoever is on it knows very well that there'll be no one around the slips there this late after dark."

Michael guided the station wagon at a boat's pace along the road that skirted the ocean. Then he turned in at the marina where mainmasts crowded the skyline.

Silently the group watched the boat ride through the clearing fog and slip softly, expertly into mooring.

As the skipper tied his craft by lantern light, the watchers could see the boat distinctly, an eighteen-foot, bright blue sloop. Printed on its side in dark blue letters were the words PELICANO III.

Robin, following close, looked in vain for Matt's familiar face. The owner of the boat, who wasn't much older than Michael, angrily questioned the police chief.

"What's the big idea? Is there a warrant out for me? Why the reception committee? I just stayed out too long on a practice run. Got a little off course, I guess. I never expected a claque like this. Who are you?"

"Who are you?" the chief asked sternly.

Robin waited for the young man's answer, her face mirroring the disappointment she felt. He couldn't know anything about Nugget. He wasn't any thief. Then her eye caught the pelican's outline on the drooping sail. Was there any connection with that other crudely drawn pelican?

She wondered about it even as she heard the boy saying, "My name is Benz, Malcolm Benz. San Diego Boat Club. I'm in these waters for the regatta, sir, this week at Monteleone. What's up?"

The chief's face fell. He shrugged and turned to the young people who stood around him.

"Can you prove it?" Michael asked, close by Robin's side.

"Do I have to?" the young man's face reddened again.

"I believe so," Michael insisted. "Is it a regular regatta, this one you're going to compete in?"

"Nope. For your information it's to be staged for some motion picture with Moira Rafferty in it. I don't remember the name of the picture. Does that satisfy you?"

"I guess it'll have to. You see, I'm Michael Hunter and my father is directing the picture. This is Moira Rafferty with us. It won't take long to explain to you why we were so steamed up. It was this way. . . ."

When Michael finished, the young man, laughing, shook hands with everyone. He had a special few words for Moira. "This is the third bright blue *Pelicano* I've owned. It's the nearest I've ever come to being arrested. I'll see you at the regatta, Moira."

The police chief seemed the most upset of all. With a brief apology to the skipper of the sloop, he hurried the little girls ahead of him toward Michael's station wagon.

When they were once again under way, Kevin spoke. "I always told you that stupid drawing on the corral didn't mean a thing. Nugget just wandered away."

"Nugget's not that kind of a horse and you know it. No matter what you say, Kevin, Mindy and I both know that blue drawing on the corral was a clue. You'll find out we're right, too."

"That will be the day."

"Clue or no clue," the chief said sternly, "the next time you kids will have to be more sure of yourselves before you get me out on such a chase. I felt plenty flattened when that guy identified himself. I should think you and Mindy would feel silly, too, Mike. Your own father's invited guest. . . ."

"I do, Chief. I feel about six inches high right now. I guess the rest of us do, too."

"I don't!" Robin said positively. "I feel just the size I am, five feet. I'll run down every clue I come across till Nugget is found. I only hope it isn't too late when we do find him." Her voice broke in a sob.

"Well, bully for you!" the chief said unexpectedly. "Count me in, Robin. If Sheriff Jackson is on the trail of the horse he's as good as found. Good night, kids."

After Michael had taken Judy home, he let the Kanes off at the gate. It had been a long day and a happy one in spite of the constant worry in the back of Robin's mind and the disappointment of the *Pelicano III*.

"Michael will pick you up around nine tomorrow morning," Mindy called. "Won't you, Michael? Manuela's expecting you for breakfast, remember—a Spanish breakfast, she said. So don't eat a bite before you come. Remember!"

8. *On the Track of Something*

AT MINDY'S low, white stone and timber beach house, Manuela came down the steps to meet Robin and Kevin. Mindy and Moira were close behind.

"The little *muchacha,* she did not come with you?" Manuela asked.

"No, Manuela. She was so sorry. She had accepted an invitation to go with Judy and her parents to San Francisco. She said she did hope you'd have corn popovers with honey for Moira. Do you?"

Manuela put her finger to her lips and smiled. "Wait, Robin. We see. Amy and Judy will go to

Chinatown in San Francisco. They like that."

"They will, and bring presents for everyone. Oh, we're going to eat on the terrace! I love it!"

No matter how often Robin visited Mindy's home and walked the long steps that led to the sandy beach, each time she was overwhelmed with its beauty. Today a gentle swell rippled in from the horizon to send tiny whitecaps against the shore.

To the left, a long rose garden spread its perfumed length in front of a sapling wall dripping with multicolored fuchsias. In front of the roses, white stocks, blue delphiniums, shasta daisies, pink geraniums, and green and white ivy circled the swimming pool, its rectangular blue mirroring an almost cloudless sky.

"We've been out here since early morning, Mindy and I," Moira said. "There was a cloud of blue butterflies . . . a miracle! They're all gone now. Even in Ireland where fuchsias grow wild in a tangle on the hills there isn't such beauty. See what Manuela has done to the table. She wouldn't let us do a thing."

A long wrought iron table was spread with cobalt blue table mats. Cranberry-colored napkins matched the sturdy Mexican glass goblets while in the center a copper bowl spilled luscious peaches, purple grapes, and golden apples.

"You sit here, please, Robin, then Michael, then Moira, Kevin, and Mindy." As Manuela spoke she placed small plates in front of each one. "Fruit," she said. "I bring your breakfast."

"Isn't it a perfect movie setting?" Moira asked as she peeled a juicy peach. "Isn't it to be part of *The Changeling?* It's all so beautiful. Have you made any shots here?"

"It's part of almost every picture my father directs," Mindy answered just a little sadly. "And everyone who visits here says, 'What a perfect movie setting!' "

Michael stripped a small bunch of grapes, smiled across the table at his sister and said, "What's the difference? We can always go to the Kanes'."

"At the Kanes' you'll never get food like this," Robin said. "Oh, Manuela, you did make corn popovers, and you did make peppered eggs!"

She helped herself to scrambled eggs striped with red pimentos, then added thin broiled ham fresh from the Rancho Lucia smokehouse.

Manuela—tall, stately Doña Manuela Avila, late

of her ancestral home Rancho Lucia—smiled hospitably as she took the platter from guest to guest. There was a great affection between the gracious housekeeper and Michael and Mindy. She filled a small part of the place in their lives left so void by the death of their mother. Robin knew that the Hunters had crept into Manuela's heart, too, to fill a need, keenly felt by the last of a long line of Avilas.

Manuela kept the Hunter home as her wealthy Spanish ancestors had once kept their home in the Santa Lucia foothills. When drought and cattle disease had brought near financial ruin and one by one the men of her family had died, Manuela had held her head high even with a broken heart. The beauty that now surrounded her had healed that break in a measure. She was not just housekeeper for the Hunter family. Michael and Mindy were her charges and their father her responsibility. It worked smoothly and created a homelike atmosphere.

They had just finished eating when Mr. Hunter and Mr. Rafferty drove in from the drive that skirted the ocean. Mr. Hunter called out to the patio, "Any coffee left, Manuela?"

Moira ran to throw her arms around the neck of

tall handsome Tim Rafferty. His bright Irish eyes twinkled as they raced around the table in greeting to his daughter's new friends.

Manuela made room quickly for the two men, poured cups of fragrant coffee, and pushed the jug of yellow cream within their reach.

"Are you having a good time, Moira?" Mr. Rafferty asked. "Don't answer. I can see it in your face. It's good you're having this playtime. The devils have been after us this morning, eh?" He smiled at Mr. Hunter.

"Does that mean there has been word of the calves . . . of Nugget?" Robin asked quickly, but Mr. Hunter shook his head.

"No. Other business worries. No news of El Gato and his gang."

"They skipped out entirely," Tim Rafferty added.

"It's like a trick the little people in your country would do, isn't it?" Kevin asked.

"Indeed it is, Kevin."

"Only there aren't any leprechauns in Ireland—"

"Oh, but there are. You're talking to a man who knows."

"My daddo does know," Moira said quickly. "And

don't ever deny the little people, Kevin, you with your Irish name. It's bad luck for sure."

"Have *you* ever seen one?" Kevin persisted.

"No, but my daddo has. Tell them."

"It was this way, then," Tim Rafferty began. He crossed his legs, brought out an old well-smoked briar pipe and filled it. Then he lit it and settled back. "It was when I was a boy in County Kerry where we now live—the very same place—but it was wilder then. The little people don't like it when land is plowed up. It sometimes destroys their wee houses. They build them under gorse bushes, and they're never seen till a plow or sickle lays them out."

"Daddo. Go on with the story."

"Yes. I was but a boy, as I said. I'd snared a rabbit for our cook to make rabbit stew. It wasn't hurt at all, for I hadn't that kind of a snare, but it struggled like mad in my arms. I'd tightened my hold when I heard an angry little voice saying over and over again, 'Let the creature go! Let the creature go!'

"Now I wasn't intending to drop a rabbit I'd been all morning chasing on the heath. I said so out loud. Then when I looked around there was no one to be seen. Again I heard the voice, angrier this time, saying, 'Let the creature go!'

"At my feet stood the reddest-faced, angriest little man I'd ever seen in all my life. He had on a green jacket, he did, and a red cap atop his head. He was bursting with fury and kept putting up his doubled fists for me to fight. 'Put the creature down!' he ordered me again. 'I'll not,' I said, the wonder in me growing bigger and bigger, for there stood the only leprechaun I'd ever seen or likely ever would see. Indeed, the wonder was so great that before I knew it, I'd loosened my hold on the rabbit and it scampered away.

" 'Now, look what you've made me do!' I cried. This time it was I who was angry. When I looked down, though, there was no one there at all. He'd vanished, green jacket, red hat and all. And to this day—"

"You've never seen another, have you, Daddo? See, though, Kevin, there *are* little people in Ireland."

"Wasn't there just a chance that the little man never was there?" Kevin asked, laughing.

"It's plain you're not Irish," Tim Rafferty replied. "It's only the Irish that ever see the little people."

Robin's face was serious. "I can believe anything after the way Nugget vanished."

"And the cattle," Mr. Hunter added. "I wish it might be leprechauns who took them. We might be able to cope with the little people. It was a good story, Tim. It grows harder and harder all the time for me to remember I was ever a boy. What do you plan to do today, son?" he asked Michael.

"We thought Moira might want to go to Point Lobos and the Big Sur. She's told us so much about the rocky coast of Ireland we'd like to have her see our own wild coast. What's the matter, Robin?"

"Nothing, Michael. I just thought . . . well, if we're going to Point Lobos we could go by way of the ranch, then across to the coast at Breakwater. That's where we last heard of the calves. Maybe they just might be able to tell us something more."

"Oh, ho . . . well, why not?" Mr. Hunter asked. "Robin's sleuthing mind won't be satisfied till she's checked on Sheriff Jackson. You could go to Breakwater, then back to Pacific Point by way of the Sur and Point Lobos. Tim, let's go over that script again. Have a good time all of you. Don't get your hopes up, Robin. After Nick, who runs the restaurant at Breakwater, saw the trucks and men, they must have taken to the air. Life is filled with disappointments, Robin. There are three more palominos for you to ride at the ranch."

"There's just one Nugget," Robin answered sadly. "I do miss him so."

Mr. Hunter took Tim Rafferty's arm, and they went to his study.

Kevin and Robin thanked Manuela. Then, with Michael and Mindy and Moira, they raced for the station wagon. Robin's face was beaming. She was going to *do* something to try to solve the mystery of Nugget's disappearance.

"There's a queer old landing near Breakwater," Michael said when the wagon was under way. "The trip won't be all lost even if we don't learn anything about El Gato. Years ago when Father Serra was building his mission along the California coast, Spanish boats used to unload men and provisions at that landing. Later, fishermen took it over. It's abandoned now, I believe."

"Too many ships were wrecked there long ago,"

Mindy said. "Daddy said if we'd go up real high on the cliffs above Breakwater and look down into the ocean, we might still be able to see the wreck of an old ship."

"Gol!" Kevin exclaimed. "Maybe there's Spanish gold in the hold."

Michael hooted. "Two generations of people have had the same idea, Kev. Ever since scuba divers have started exploring the waters off this coast, some of them have been down there from time to time for a look around. They didn't find a thing."

"Somebody *did* find over a million dollars' worth of Spanish gold and jewelry in the ocean right near Cape Kennedy, and not too long ago. There were more Spanish ships wrecked on this coast than on the Atlantic. I'd just like to give it a try."

"Not today, please," Robin begged. *"Please,* may we go right to Breakwater?"

"We can try it," Kevin said, disappointed, "but two bits says the sheriff won't even be there."

"I hope he isn't. I want to go to Nick's restaurant. I want to talk to Nick himself. Okay, Michael?"

"Okay, Robin. We can stop there for hamburgers, if you'd like."

"Hamburgers, after that breakfast!" Moira gasped.

"Well, we can't just walk into the man's place and not buy something. He'll be a lot more likely to answer questions we ask if we're customers. He's probably been questioned a lot already."

Michael searched his pockets. "Does anybody have any money? I only have a dollar."

"My allowance is always spent long before I get it," Kevin said airily. "I don't have a cent. But I do have an appetite."

"I have a dollar and twenty cents," Robin said. "Mindy has a dollar."

"I *never* carry any money," Moira moaned. "Oh, dear!"

"Forget it," Kevin said. "Hamburgers won't cost three dollars. If they do, some of you who aren't hungry can just take Cokes."

The hamburgers at Nick's were good, so good that even Moira ate one hungrily. Nick was talkative and wanted to help. He just couldn't. The men, he said—one of them undeniably El Gato—had eaten at his restaurant. Outside, there had been several truckloads of bawling calves. He didn't know how many trucks and, since his place had been crowded at the time, he didn't know how many other men were with El Gato.

"Nope, no palominos, no horse of any kind," he said in answer to Robin's quick question. "I know, because I'm crazy about palominos. If there'd been one outside I'd have gone out to see him."

"Did you overhear any of El Gato's conversation?" Robin asked hopefully. "Did you hear him say anything about where he was heading?"

"No, miss. I've told that to the sheriff every time he's asked me. I'm sorry. I told you the place was full. I don't listen to what people are talking about in my restaurant. I wish I had, this time. I'm sorry."

"Well, that's that," Kevin said when they left the building. "Robin, you might just as well resign yourself to letting Sheriff Jackson make his own search and accept what he says."

"I can't do that." Robin looked around in frustration. "I wonder if there's *anyone* I can talk to."

"Nobody the sheriff hasn't asked," Kevin said. "This expedition is supposed to be fun, Robin, for Moira. It's about as funny as a funeral."

Robin turned quickly to Moira. "That's so. Forgive me. I know what we'll do. We'll go up on the cliffs and see if we can see the wreck. You'd like that, wouldn't you, Moira?"

Moira nodded. "I want to do anything the rest of you want to do, and forget about me not having fun. Everything I do with you is fun. I haven't been with anyone my own age for so long."

"Let's go, then," Michael said and led the way.

The cliffs on the ocean side were high and steep, but the approach from the rear was gradual. It did not take them long to reach the top and gaze out at the broad sweep of the ocean below them.

Rocks and weathered planks led out into the water for several hundred feet. Most of the planks were rotting. From the height of the cliffs, however, the young people could see signs of some attempt—quite recent—to repair the piling and strengthen the passageway out to deeper water.

"It looks as though someone may be thinking of using this place again," Michael said. "Maybe fishing boats."

"Yeah," Kevin agreed. "Fishing's getting better I guess. Say—aren't there some men out there on the wharf? Something's moving. Sure enough, it's men. Look closely."

Robin didn't answer. She was gazing fixedly at the ocean below the wharf. She scrambled a short way down the cliff to get a better view. Then she motioned excitedly for the others to join her.

"See that?" She pointed. "Did you ever see a boat like that?"

"It's not a boat," Michael said. "It's a kind of barge. Looks like its equipped for ocean freight. What's the matter now, Robin?"

"It's what those men said—Mindy, remember?" Robin's voice was high and shrill. "El Gato and Jake—up there on the mountain. Remember what they said? 'Boats don't wait for anyone'! How *could* I have forgotten? Let's run. We've got to get to a telephone. We've got to talk to the sheriff here in Breakwater, too."

"First you've got to tell us what it's all about. Do you see something we don't see?" Kevin asked.

"I know what she's talking about," Mindy said solemnly. "How could we both be so dumb? We heard El Gato with our own ears say something about boats. Why didn't we remember it?"

"Yes," Robin cried and ran down the hill, beckoning the others to follow. "Yes, that's it," she called

back. "That's why the trucks disappeared. That's why no one else down the coast saw the calves—or Nugget. They put them on a barge and towed them, sure as you're born."

"What could they hope to gain by that?" Kevin asked breathlessly as they piled into the station wagon for the run to the sheriff's office in Breakwater.

"Just exactly what they did gain," Robin answered. "Can't you go any faster, Michael? They disappeared, Kevin. Nobody ever thought of ocean freight because nobody is used to such a thing around here."

"Unless the sheriff's dead and buried he should have known there was freighting from that landing. Just wait till we talk to him! Boy!" Kevin was disgusted.

"Sure I know there's freighting from that old wharf," the sheriff at Breakwater told them. "It's been repaired by a group of Sicilians from back in the vegetable garden country. They carry produce and fruit from the valley that way. It's a lot cheaper. Nobody's ever carried livestock. The runway wouldn't hold up one animal, to say nothing of fifty or more."

"Did you ever ask them?" Robin insisted.

"I don't have to ask them. They truck in lettuce and grapes and artichokes and row them out to the barge. They're here in the vicinity of Breakwater about an hour getting the stuff on board, and then they're gone."

"There's someone down on the wharf now. Three men," Robin said. "We didn't see any produce or fruit anyplace. There's a queer-looking craft out in the ocean. Don't you want to go back with us and question the men? It won't do any harm."

"It won't do any good either, but here I go, just to satisfy you. What are you, Robin, some kind of a detective?"

"You said it," Kevin answered. "She's Robin, the girl Sherlock. Mindy's her Dr. Watson. Say, what do you know, she may just be on the track of something!"

Robin *was* on the track of something. Under questioning, the Sicilians said they had loaded calves just a few days before. They had improvised a loading ramp under El Gato's supervision, and the calves—seventy or more of them—were on the way to a town just this side of the border. From there they would be trucked across. How could they, themselves, ever know the calves were stolen? The man, El Gato, had said he wanted cheaper transportation, and the Sicilians provided it. There never was any question about the barges being strong enough to carry livestock. The only question had been how to get them on the barges. El Gato had found a way.

Chagrined, the sheriff went back to his office. There was still time to apprehend the men and calves at the landing point north of Tia Juana. By telephone he talked with Sheriff Jackson, and the machinery was set in motion. The calves were as good as on their way back—or so the sheriff at Breakwater told Robin.

The thing he didn't tell her was any news of Nugget. He didn't tell her, nor did the Sicilians, nor did Nick at the restaurant. From the time Nugget had disappeared from the corral with only the drawing of the flying blue pelican left behind as a clue, not one person questioned had seen or heard of the golden horse. No one had seen him but Matt—and where was Matt?

9. *"I'll Be Back"*

EARLY THE NEXT morning the doorbell rang in Robin's home and she went to answer it. When she saw Mr. Hunter standing at the entrance, her face lighted up. "It's news of Nugget, isn't it? Were El Gato and Jake flown back here? They told you where we can find Nugget, didn't they?"

"No, Robin. It's not that kind of news at all. It's all very puzzling. May I come in?"

"Oh, yes! Goodness, yes! Mom, Dad! It's Mr. Hunter. Will you have some coffee? We were just having our breakfast. What is so puzzling?"

Mr. Hunter sat in the chair Robin's father put at the table for him, and Mrs. Kane poured coffee.

"It's a pretty strange thing, Robin. I've already questioned Mindy. She and Moira and Michael have gone to the ranch. I'd like to take you and Kevin out with me— Well, to get back to what's puzzling. You heard El Gato and Jake talk about how they stole my calves, didn't you? You told us that the other night."

"Yes. We told you everything just the way it happened. Except we *did* forget about the calves being taken by boat."

"That's the reason I'm wondering. You may possibly have forgotten something else. Maybe something Matt said about *selling* the calves to El Gato and Jake."

"Selling the calves? Matt? Oh, no. No, they never once mentioned anything like that. They were trying to get Matt to help them load the calves *they* had stolen. Don't you remember I heard them tell Matt that there were more calves they could get—that they wanted to get them before branding season? I do remember so well hearing El Gato say, 'No brand, no proof.' Why are you asking me this?"

"Because El Gato and Jake have a paper with Matt's signature on it showing that he sold seventy Hereford calves to them on the very date my calves were stolen."

"He couldn't! It's a forgery!"

"I don't think it is, Robin. It looks to me as though Matt is the real thief."

"Are they going to let those rustlers go?" Kevin asked. "It's a great big lie they're telling, isn't it, Robin?"

"It *is*. Oh, it's all so mixed up. Mr. Hunter, I know as well as I know I'm alive that those men are the thieves and they're trying to put it all on Matt."

"He was involved with them," Mr. Kane said. "Perhaps Mr. Hunter is right in thinking he may be the one most responsible."

"I know he was mixed up in it, Daddy. You should have heard the way he talked to them, though, up there on the mesa. They *made* him go with them. Oh, what am I going to do? Are they going to let El Gato and Jake go, Mr. Hunter?"

"I'm not sure what the sheriff will do, Robin. Will you come with me and talk to him? The men are still in custody. Sheriff Jackson will be at the ranch when we get there. I'm sure he'll want to hear the story over again from you and Mindy."

"Shall I go, Mom?" Robin asked, then explained to Mr. Hunter, "I'd told Mom I'd take Amy and Judy to the beach."

"Why not come to the ranch instead? I can take them with us. Amy always loves to see the animals."

"Let's do it this way," Mrs. Kane said. "You and Kevin go with Mr. Hunter, Robin. He's anxious to have you talk with Sheriff Jackson. Later in the day I'll pick up Judy, and we'll all go out. Daddy too, maybe."

At the ranch Mindy and Robin repeated the conversation they had overheard among El Gato and Jake and Matt. They told their stories separately and agreed on every word.

"El Gato's a slippery one," Sheriff Jackson said when the girls had finished talking. "Every sheriff between here and the border knows that he's a bad one. The big job is to pin anything on him. Now, I believe what the girls are telling me. What can I do, though, when the rustlers have that bill of sale? You can't put guys in prison for stealing something they can prove they bought."

"Can't you possibly hold them for a while?" Robin asked desperately. "I just know something will happen soon. If we can only find Matt! If we can only find Jeff, even, he'll be able to tell us something. We know Matt took him someplace that night. I think he took Nugget to the same place in spite of what he told El Gato about turning him loose. Oh, dear, isn't it dreadful?"

"It's tough," Sheriff Jackson admitted. "There's one thing I can do legally, Robin. I can hold those two men for at least forty-eight hours. Then if nothing definite turns up I'll have to let them go. I'd hate to do it, but you see how it is, don't you, girls?"

Mindy nodded her head resignedly. Not Robin. Her head went up and her chin squared.

"We have forty-eight hours to prove those men are lying," she said. "We have forty-eight hours to find Matt or Jeff or someone! Let's go talk to Moira and the boys."

"Cheer up!" Sheriff Jackson called as the girls left. "My men are all over those mountains. They're bound to come up with something. Don't you kids try any funny business. We don't want any lost girls to complicate things."

After a few moments Mr. Hunter left them and returned to Pacific Point, saying he would be back again in the evening.

Robin and Mindy found Moira, Michael, and Kevin loading their ponies with picks and shovels and specimen cases.

"We thought we'd go up in the hills—you know, up near the mesa, and see if we could pick up some jadeite, maybe some amethysts or garnets for Moira . . . up there near the mesa," Kevin repeated, stressing the last word.

"Oh, I catch! You darling!" Robin cried and hugged her brother.

"Hey, lay off that!" he said, his face reddening. "If we do some prospecting, who's to know what we're really prospecting for? We've saddled Bueno and Sugar for you girls. Want to get started?"

For answer Robin swung herself into the saddle, pushed her knees against Bueno's flanks and was off, flying across the flat land toward the hills.

At the edge of the forest she waited impatiently

while the rest of her group rode up. Then, with Michael in the lead on his spotted pony Calico, they started up the trail single file.

"It's a special day!" Robin called out happily. "I know it's special. Something wonderful is going to happen on a day like this. See if it doesn't."

As far as they could see, pines and great live oaks spread softly back from the hillsides. There were outcroppings of rock and ragged thorn bushes as the trail through the woods emerged crookedly at the cliffs. Riding could be dangerous, as Robin and Mindy well remembered. Now, in dry weather, with sure-footed ponies, they were soon over the ridge and into the valley.

Here a trout stream gushed through the rocks to disappear in a shadowed subterranean tunnel. The boys stopped, unloaded their shovels and picks, and helped the girls tie their horses to low-hanging branches.

"We'll have to take something back with us to show we've been rock-hunting," Kevin said. "Say, look at this, will you?"

He held up a rock his pick had uncovered, a lovely shade of translucent pink quartz. Moira took it, rubbed it on her blue jeans and held it up to the light. "It's beautiful! At home we have a little lamp with a pink quartz base."

"If you think that's something, wait till we dig up a piece of jade for you," Michael said. "Did you wear your jade ring, Mindy? Show it to Moira. Maybe we can find something like it for her. Think so, Kevin?"

Kevin nodded and went on digging industriously. The girls watched, fascinated. All but Robin. Her eyes were fixed on the fringe of trees around them, constantly seeking—looking for the glint of a palomino's coat, searching through the underbrush for a ragged coat that could be Matt's.

Gradually, as the voices of her friends rose in playful conversation, Robin circled farther and farther away from them—searching.

"No one but me knows the hurt that's inside of me till I find Matt and he clears all this puzzle and Nugget is back," she thought. "I'd rather not laugh and talk with the others any more. I want to be by myself and I want to find some clue. The others don't honestly think Nugget is here in the hills. I do. He's so much a part of my heart that I know

when he's close to me. I can feel it clear into the middle of my bones."

Into Robin's conversation with herself a dull tap-tapping intruded. She sensed it almost without being aware of it. Then she stopped short and listened.

Tap. Tap. Tap. Tap.

It sounded like the ping of a hammer or chisel on rock. It couldn't be coming from where the boys were. They were so far away she couldn't even hear the boisterous song of the rushing trout stream.

Tap. Tap. Tap.

There it was again.

Robin parted the buckeye bushes and went around a big boulder that obstructed her view. There, working away at a stone outcropping, she saw a whiskered old man at work. He was chipping away small bits of rock, looking at them with his shoe-button eyes, and adding them to a half-full paper bag. As he worked, he glanced about furtively, apparently not wanting to be seen.

Robin was frightened. There was something otherworldly about the old man. She drew back into the shelter of the boulder, peeping out now and then to watch. As he added rock after rock to his paper bag he laughed out loud, a crazy splintery laugh that turned Robin's blood to ice.

Then, as a final rock rattled into the paper bag, he turned the bag around. Robin's heart stood still. On the side of the bag, plain in the bright sunlight, a queer blue scrawl stood out. A flying pelican! The one mysterious clue to Nugget's disappearance!

With another quick glance around, the old man scrambled out of his digging pit and up the bank. Robin scarcely had time to hide in the buckeye clump. He *must* be able to hear her thumping heart, she thought.

Wherever he was going, she had to follow. There was no time to run back for her brother or friends. She would lose sight of the old man altogether. She must move *now* to find Nugget. For this old man knew where the silver and gold palomino could be found. That queer scrawl on his specimen bag wasn't there just by chance.

Slowly, quietly, Robin followed. She followed the old man over a primitive trail that led back into the woods. Her feet padding softly, she pushed aside branches, releasing them gently so the old man's quick ears couldn't possibly hear their returning swish. Once a dead twig crackled and he turned, sharp as a fox. His ears pointed up under his bushy hair. His eyes darted across the distance between Robin and himself and almost caught sight of her.

The trail had been crudely made. Branches were cut back and underbrush trimmed. Crude as it was, it had been followed, evidently, quite often by man and horse.

"He's going home," Robin thought. "I have to follow him. Oh, I do wish Michael and Kevin were here!"

Stopping now and then to look back, as though his old ears picked up the sound of somebody following, the prospector went on. The woods were closer and more dense now. The path wandered crookedly. Finally, when Robin thought she would surely be lost if she went farther, she saw an old shack in the middle of a clearing.

The old man's footsteps quickened as he neared it. So did Robin's.

"He can't disappear into that shack before I have a chance to ask him about Nugget," she thought. "Or till I find the answer to that blue pelican on the bag he carries."

He did disappear, though, around the house and on, apparently, far back of it. Robin watched, not knowing what to do till she saw him reappear without the bag, then lift the latch on the front door of the shack.

Quickly she looked back over the trail she had covered. "I'll have a head start on him if he turns out to be mean," she thought. "Now is the time for me to call to him. He *must* tell me of Matt and Nugget. I know he can if he will."

Impulsively she called out and the old man whirled and saw her. He picked up a club and snarled, "Get out! Get out! Who's with you, girl? Get out, I say! Get away from my house!"

"I can't go. You must help me. Everything depends on you. Please wait . . . answer me!"

The old man reached through the door of the house for his gun. "You get out of here! Hear me? I don't answer no questions for nobody. Git!"

"Oh, *please* tell me. Where is my horse, Nugget? My beautiful palomino! Where is Matt? Where is his boy Jeff?"

With a wild cry the old man lunged forward with his gun held high. "Who are you? I ain't never heard of no horse. I don't know what you're talkin' about. Who sent you?" He stopped still, raised his gun. "Where'd you come from, girl? Why do you ask me those questions?"

"Because I just know you can tell me the answers."

Robin's voice was strong and clear. The certainty that she was at last on the trail of Nugget and Matt buoyed her up, gave her strength. "Because I saw that drawing of a blue pelican on your bag of rocks. Whoever put it there can tell me where Matt is and where I can find my horse, Nugget. Did *you* draw it?"

The old man's face was fiery red, contorted with anger. "I ain't tellin' you nor any other body a thing," he said. "I'll give you just two minutes to git out of here. Git down that trail and don't you never come back. You'll never git near this house. I can promise you that."

With blazing eyes he shouldered his rifle, aimed it into the air and fired.

"Next time it'll be pointin' at you or any other busybodies you've a mind to bring with you. I mean business."

"So do I," Robin cried defiantly. "So do I. I'll be back, for I know where my horse is, and Matt and Jeff. The blue pelican gave you away, old man. I'll be back."

10. *In the Dust of the Trail*

ONCE OUT OF sight of the shack, Robin broke into a run, crashing through the underbrush that grew out over the trail. It seemed as though her legs couldn't carry her fast enough back to her brother and friends to report what she had found.

She had gone only about halfway to the digging pit where she had left the others, when she heard shouting and the sound of ponies' hoofs.

"Robin! Robin!" Michael's voice cried. "Can you hear me, Robin? Answer me! Are you all right, Robin? Answer me!"

"I'm all right!" Robin called, her voice clear and jubilant. "Just wait till I tell you what I found. I'm sure the old man has Nugget, and maybe Matt and Jeff. Nugget's back there in that grove somewhere, I know, but the old man wouldn't let me go near the shack. He'll shoot us if we get in range of his rifle. We have to be awfully careful, Michael."

"Robin, calm yourself! What are you talking about? Did someone shoot at you? We heard the shot. That's why we came after you. You must have been seeing things. Nugget? He couldn't be here. Did you actually see him?" Mindy put her arm around her friend to quiet her. Then, as Robin grew more calm, and her heart assumed its normal beat, she grinned triumphantly and told her story to her brother and friends.

When she had finished, Michael fingered the lasso that hung on the pommel of his saddle. "Was he alone? Was there anyone there but the old man?"

"I didn't see anyone. I'm certain Matt is there. Jeff, too. And there was something in the air that told me Nugget was near. I could sense it. If Matt isn't there then that old man knows where he is. I don't think he looks like an artist, but someone drew that pelican on the sack that held his rocks. It's all so puzzling. We *have* to go back there and see what we can find. Sheriff Jackson will only hold those men forty-eight hours, you know. I'm positive we can find something at that old shack that will help us."

"Then let's go," Michael said. "Ride back of me, Kevin. You'll have to point out the way, Robin."

"He's a terribly fierce old man. If he sees us first and shoots. . . ." Her voice broke. "Let's be awfully, awfully quiet. I'm sure he thinks he's scared me off—that I'll be afraid to go back. He may be trying to hide Jeff and Nugget and Matt somewhere else. It would have to be farther back in the woods, though, otherwise he'd have to come out on this trail. Maybe we can leave the ponies here and sneak up through the trees away from the trail. Keep it in sight. Do you think we can?"

"I know we're going to do it. How about it, Kev? You girls stay out of it, though."

Robin's protest was quick and clear. "Not a chance! Do you have your lasso, Michael? If we see him before he knows we're around, you'll get him. Do be quiet, now!"

Michael led the way, Kevin right back of him, then Robin, Mindy, and Moira. Single file they skulked, Indian fashion, through the trees, around the rocks and underbrush.

Near the house, back in the clearing, they could hear the old man still sputtering. As they drew near enough to hear, they laughed quietly at his monologue.

"Darned girl! Nosy, like all women. Didn't take long to send her kitin' out o' here." He broke off with a coarse, trembling laugh. "There ain't nobody goin' to get into this here place of mine except them as belongs here. Nosy, that's what she was. But I scairt her. Yep." He fingered his gun in the bend of his arm. "You and me scairt the daylights out o' her. She won't come back."

"Oh, yes, she will!" Robin sang out, and the boys in front of her charged forward.

The old man turned in frenzy. Before he could shoulder his gun, Michael, with a war whoop, swung his lasso around his head, let go. The rope sang through the air, looped about the old prospector, bringing him easily, softly to the ground. His gun flew out of his arms, landing twenty feet away.

Quickly Kevin and the girls tied his hands and feet with the length of the lasso. He was a wiggling bundle of fury, but he couldn't loosen a knot. "I'll kill you! I'll kill you all! Every tarnation one of you!" he cried in frustration.

"Oh, no, you won't," Michael told the old man. "You won't shoot anyone. You're tied up now, a nice little bundle for the sheriff when we go back down to the ranch. Before that, though, we're going to look around your place a bit. We think you may have something or someone around we'd like very much to see or talk to. How about it—want to tell us?"

Furiously muttered oaths were the only answer Michael received. "You'll pay for this, young 'uns. See if you don't. You and that girl. What do you want of a poor old man, anyway? I ain't got nothin' you'd want."

"We'll have to be sure of that ourselves," Michael answered. "We're sorry you can't show us around, but we'll do the very best we can without a guide. Squirm away. Don't be so quick with the trigger next time. We won't be gone long, I'm sure. Come on, Kev, Robin, Mindy. Say, Moira, I'll bet you

never counted on anything like this, did you?"

"No. I'm glad I'm here, though. This is real. Maybe I can help my daddo write a script from it some day. This part of it, anyway. Heavens, Michael, I never saw anything like the way you lassoed him! Say, do you suppose we can go inside the shack?"

"I suppose we're going to. We don't have a search warrant, and he could kick up a fuss about that. Something tells me, though, that he'll be busy enough thinking about other things. Here we are!"

Kevin opened the door, stepped back, and gallantly motioned to the girls to go inside.

"Careful!" Michael warned. "He might have a partner around the corner."

"Not that mean old geek," Kevin said. "Anybody would be afraid to get near him."

Robin gazed about the room. "Look at all these papers all over the floor . . . yes . . . look at them! Gosh, just look at them! Every one of them is covered with drawings of that flying blue pelican! Now, Kevin Kane, do you still think that isn't a clue? Glory! That's why the pelican was on that bag."

"It may be a clue but it hasn't led us to anything

yet but a snarling old bully."

"Maybe he's the one who drew the pelicans," Mindy said slowly. "No . . . he couldn't be. Just look at all those papers!"

Moira bent to pick one up and then, without a word, held it flat for the rest to see. Down in the corner they saw printed in big childish letters the name "Jeff."

"Jeff's here! Matt's here." Robin cried. "Nugget's someplace. See that, Michael? See it, Kevin? Jeff's the one who drew those pictures. But, no—that means Matt stole Nugget. Jeff must have been with him when he did it—sat on the corral fence, maybe, waiting, while Matt stole my darling Nugget. Oh, that's terrible! Then maybe Matt did steal the calves after all, and sold them—"

"Hey, Robin, slow down," Kevin warned. "You and Mindy overheard that conversation between Matt and Jake and El Gato, don't forget that."

Robin nodded her head, perplexed. "Yes, that's right. I mustn't forget it. It's all so mixed up and mysterious, though, I'm not sure sometimes what I did hear." She stopped, looked around. "This house is a mess, isn't it? Things all over the floor.

Clothes hanging on chairs and—say, those clothes are too big for that little old man, aren't they?"

Robin took a coat and trousers from the back of a chair. She held them up. "He could get into these twice." Then her eyes opened wide in amazement. "They're Matt's clothes. They're Jeff's father's clothes. I think we'd better look around outside a little."

A conglomeration of junk surrounded the house, filled the yard. Most of it was rusted beyond any hope of practical use. There was an old harness, machinery for washing out gold dust, broken chairs, even an old wooden pump.

The young people picked their way across it. From the front yard where he lay tied, the old man saw them and called out new threats. "You just stay away from there. Hear me? You go farther and you'll run into a wildcat. Sure as you're born. There's one out there. Yes, sir. Stay back here in the yard if you value your lives."

"Is there something there in the woods that you don't want us to see?" Robin called back to him. "You know you don't have a pet wildcat. Maybe there is something else. Let's find out, Michael.

Isn't that another old shack back there—and a barn? Oh, Michael, it is! And what would be in that barn? Nugget! Oh, Nugget! Nugget? Nugget? Can you hear me calling you, Nugget?"

From inside the barn a loud snuffle and a sharp whinny answered Robin!

With a cry of joy she ran to him. The others stood back, waiting and listening to Robin's low voice speaking to the palomino.

As they waited and watched, a little boy ran out from the shack next to the barn. Matt's little boy, Jeff!

"Is my daddy here?" he cried. "I heard people. Did my daddy send for me? Where is he?"

Michael caught the boy in his arms, but the child's eager eyes went past Michael's face, searching. "Did you bring my daddy with you?"

Robin heard him. She came out of the barn, leading Nugget.

"Don't you take my daddy's horse!" Jeff cried. "He told old Hardtack Jack to keep his horse and me till he'd come and get us. Hardtack Jack will shoot if he sees you."

Robin handed Nugget's rein to Mindy and knelt

down beside Jeff. "Your daddy isn't with us, Jeff. Hardtack Jack won't hurt us. He's out in the front yard. We had to tie him up. He wanted to harm us. We want to help you, Jeff, to find your daddy. Do you have any idea where he is?"

"No, ma'am, I don't. You shouldn't tie up old Hardtack Jack. He tried to be good to us. He let me stay here when my daddy was gone. Let him go. Let me go, too. I want to go where my daddy is."

"We'll take you there, if you'll just tell us where it is," Robin said soothingly. "My name is Robin. We want to help you, Jeff. Honestly we do."

"My daddy was a soldier in Viet Nam," Jeff said suddenly. "Do you know where Viet Nam is, Robin? There's an ocean and you have to go on a big plane."

"Yes?" Robin encouraged him, hoping he'd say more.

"My mama died when my daddy was in the war." His voice broke, for he really was a very little boy. Manfully brushing away his tears, he went on. "I was lonesome. I lived with my Aunt Jennie. It was in San Francisco. Then my daddy came home from the war. He couldn't find a job. I still had to live with my Aunt Jennie and there wasn't any room for me. I hope my daddy found a job and I can be with him all the time. Do you know where he is, Robin?"

"No, Jeff, I don't. I wish I did. How did you happen to be here with Hardtack Jack?"

"My daddy and I was ridin' his big horse. That horse. That's my daddy's horse. Some bad men stopped us. Then they went to sleep and my daddy brought me and his horse here and he went away. He said he had to. But he said he'd be back. It's been two whole days."

"We'll find him, honey. Just you wait and see. Are you sure he isn't here?"

Jeff shook his head vigorously. "No, ma'am. He wasn't here since he left me with Hardtack Jack. Me and his horse."

"Jeff is right," Michael told Robin. "We have been all over the place and the only sign of Matt is the clothes we saw. I guess we're just about where we were."

"Oh, no, we're not! We have Jeff and—" Robin's voice softened lovingly—"we have Nugget!"

"And about thirty-some hours to come up with

Matt—or El Gato and Jake will go free. How about that?" Kevin asked.

"We'll have to go back to the ranch and try another way to find him," Robin answered. "I know we'll find him. We can't miss after what has happened today."

"What will we do with our little friend in the front yard?" Kevin asked. "He'd never stay on a horse. He's like a can of angleworms, all squirmy."

"Then you'll have to stay here and watch him until we send a deputy back," Michael told him. "Or you can go with the girls and I'll stay. What do you want to do?"

Kevin looked at Hardtack Jack. "How about it, fella? Want some company?"

Hardtack Jack just growled. "Where you takin' the kid?"

"To Rancho Lucia. He needs some good food and milk and some clean clothes," Michael answered.

"You'll like it at the ranch, Jeff," Robin said. "There's a boy there almost the same age as you. His name is Felipe. There's a good old lazy dog, Perro. And cowboys and horses. You can stay there till we find your daddy. I know that will be soon."

"All right, Robin, if you say so. Hardtack Jack just eats biscuits. I didn't like them very well and my daddy's horse didn't like them either."

"I can't blame him, if Hardtack Jack mixed the biscuits," Kevin said. "Get going, Mike. I don't think I'll find this old geezer too entertaining. Get a deputy up here as soon as you can. Funny we haven't seen any of the sheriff's men. They're supposed to be all over the place."

"Sheriff Jackson sent them over across the canyon," Michael said. "I guess he never dreamed we'd find anyone on this side. Take it easy, Kev."

"Yeah. It's after noon now. Leave a sandwich for me out of the lunch Mamacita packed for us. I guess Jeff could stand one, too. Maybe even old Hardtack would be our guest—if he doesn't bite me when I give it to him."

"I'll stay with you if you want me to," Moira offered.

"Me, too," Mindy said.

"I'd sure like it, but I won't let you, either one of you. Nope. Go ahead. I'll just relax."

Robin slid Nugget's saddle over his back, tightened the girth and mounted. Michael swung Jeff up in front of her. Then he told her to ride on ahead, that he would follow. Nugget wasn't used to following in line as the cow ponies did.

Slowly they started down the crooked trail toward the place where it merged with the wider mountain trail. Carefully Nugget set one foot in front of the other, avoiding tree roots and shaking branches back with his beautiful head.

Robin, in the saddle, patted the big horse's flank gently. "Oh, I do love you so," she murmured. "Are you all right, Jeff?"

"Yes, Robin," the little boy answered. "I just want to find my daddy."

"Careful, Nugget!" Robin warned, and tightened her rein. "It's all right now, boy. Careful! What is it, Nugget? Did something frighten you?"

Nugget shied, looked down at the ground in front of him, stood still and would not move.

"What's the matter?" Michael called quickly to Robin.

"There's something in the path. Nugget won't go on. Can you see what it is?"

Michael dismounted, looked, then carefully helped Robin from the saddle. They bent over the bundle which was lying in the dust of the trail.

"Let *me* see. What is it?" Jeff asked.

"Hold on to the reins for me, Jeff," Robin said quietly, standing so the boy could not see the bundle on the ground. "I'll be with you in a minute."

In the faint light that came through the thick pines Robin and Michael could make out the crumpled form of a man, ragged, torn, and terribly dirty. His bare arm was thrown across his bloody face. On that arm a pelican was tattooed, sharply picked out in blue. The "bundle" that had made Nugget shy was Jeff's daddy, Matt.

Gently Michael lifted Jeff from Nugget's back and handed him to Mindy. "Turn around and go back," he said. "Wait for us in the yard where Kevin is. Tell him to come here. You and Moira stay with Jeff, please. We'll explain to you later. We'll come back for you, Jeff. Nugget stumbled and we have to look after him."

11. *An Explanation*

MATT'S BEEN HURT," Robin said, awed, in a low trembling voice. "I'm afraid he's dead. Is he, Michael?"

Michael was on his knees at Matt's side, head down, listening for breath and heartbeat. He touched Matt's chest, and the man moaned.

"He's not dead. He's almost gone, though, I'm afraid. Help me turn him over, Kevin, so he'll be more comfortable. Thanks. What did you say, Robin?"

"Isn't it terrible? Jeff's daddy. Do you suppose

we could possibly get him inside that shack and put him on the bed? Listen, he's trying to say something."

Robin lifted Matt's head ever so gently. "What is it you're trying to say, Matt?"

"Water!" he whispered hoarsely.

Robin unscrewed the cap of her canteen and tipped the bottle for him while he drank a few sips. Then she spilled a little water on her handkerchief and wiped his scratched, bleeding face. Revived, he raised himself and looked at them, then let his head fall back on Robin's arm.

"I . . . saw . . . you . . . on . . . the street . . . in Pacific Point," he said weakly. "You . . . and . . . the . . . little girl . . . and the dog. I *have* to trust you, and you, and you!" He turned his eyes to Robin, to Michael, and to Kevin.

"Those men!" he gasped. "They tried to . . . kill me! El Gato and Jake. They stole a lot of calves . . . from the ranch . . . down there. They're taking them . . . on the ocean . . . not on the highway. Tell the police! You kids get the sheriff and catch up with them!"

Matt's voice took on strength as he spoke. "There's

time to stop them before they get to the border. Hurry! I guess . . . there's . . . time."

He put his hand to his head and a bewildered look crossed his face. "I was knocked out . . . so long!"

Michael's sure hands traveled up and down Matt's arms and legs, hunting breaks. There did not seem to be any, though he was terribly bruised, with open cuts still bleeding on his legs, arms, and body. One eye was closed and his face was criss-crossed with scratches.

"I don't think there's any really serious injury," Michael said as he stood up. "Unless it could be internal. Do you hurt very much any place, fella?"

"Just about everywhere," Matt answered, trying to smile a little. "I know it isn't serious because I walked. I walked and dragged myself here from the cliff over the river in the canyon. I just had to get back here to Jeff. Where is he?"

Matt sat up, then almost toppled with dizziness. "I guess I must have passed out just as I made it back here to Hardtack Jack's trail. Where's he? Where's Jeff? How'd you ever find this place?"

When they had answered all his questions and

explained that Hardtack Jack was trussed up in the yard, and why, and that Jeff was with the girls at the shack, Matt moaned. "Set him free—Jack. He's kind of a good old man. He took me in when no one else would. He's been taking care of Jeff and—" He looked over at Nugget placidly, patiently waiting. "He took care of the horse, too. I didn't steal the palomino."

Robin looked at Michael. He looked at Kevin, then said quietly. "We might as well tell you, Matt. El Gato and Jake are in the county jail down there near the ranch. Thanks to Robin, here, and Mindy, the men were caught just before they reached the border."

Matt gasped with relief. "Then you know I didn't have anything to do with that."

"Sorry, Matt, but they have a bill of sale to show that you stole the calves and sold them to them."

Matt put his head in his hands and sat silent for a moment. "That's bad. That's awful bad. They don't have any real bill of sale. I didn't steal anything—ever!"

"That will take some explaining," Kevin said. "If you didn't steal Nugget and the calves—"

"Kevin, that can wait!" Robin said quickly. "Let's help Matt into the shack. He can tell his story when he feels stronger. Take this chocolate bar, Matt. Later we can give you some sandwiches from our lunch. Let's try and help him go back to the shack and rest. Here, take hold, Kevin . . . and Michael."

"I can't rest. You can't either. You've got to get me to El Gato and Jake. They lied. They stole those calves that belong to that ranch down there."

"My dad's ranch," Michael said.

Matt moaned. "The horse, then. He belongs to you. Because you found him here you think I stole the calves, too."

"There's plenty of evidence," Kevin said quickly. "Robin did find the horse here, with Jeff. Jeff calls Nugget 'daddy's horse.' Maybe you can tell us about that. It happens to be Mr. Hunter's palomino and was stolen from Rancho Lucia."

"Give me time," Matt begged. "Give me time and I'll begin at the beginning and tell you the whole story. I want to see Jeff."

With Michael on one side and Kevin on the other they succeeded in getting Matt to the yard where Hardtack Jack lay, still cursing. When he saw Matt he cursed louder. "You got me into this. Git this rope off me. All of you. And you, Matt, you take that kid and git outa here. I never want to see any of you again."

"Take it easy, fella," Michael said. "I think you'd better stay tied up for a while till your temper cools. We've got a lot of listening to do."

"Yeah," Kevin added. "How do we know you two aren't in cahoots? We can handle you when you're tied and Matt's down the way he is now. We'll have to hear the story first. Here comes Jeff, Matt."

The little boy ran out from the house, looked at his father, puzzled, looked again, and then ran to the outstretched arms. "How'd you get hurt, Daddy? You did come for me, didn't you, like you said? I've been good. Ask Hardtack Jack. Don't ever go away from me again, Daddy."

"I won't," Matt promised in a choking voice. "I won't again, son—ever. Let's go into the house. I've got talking to do."

In the shack, Matt gingerly stretched himself out on the dirty, bare cot. The young people got the sandwiches and passed them out, then stood to listen.

Jeff went down on his knees beside Matt.

"I *was* in the pen. That was where I met El Gato and Jake. They were about to be sprung after serving time for armed robbery. I'd been sent up for stealing a car. I never did steal it—or anything else. The guy I was riding with, hitchhiking, told me it was his car. You've got to believe me!" He looked around, his blackened eyes pleading.

"Go on, fella," Michael said.

"I *do* want to believe you," Robin said quickly. "But, oh, how *did* you get Nugget?"

"I'll have to get to that in time. I said I was in the pen and I told you the truth about how I got there. Those two, El Gato and Jake, wanted me to go in with them on a lot of jobs they'd planned after we'd all get out. I refused. Oh, it's such a long story."

"Take your time, Matt," Robin said kindly.

"Well, my wife died just before it was time for me to be let out. Her sister Jennie lives in San Francisco and she took Jeff. She took him even though there wasn't any room for him. She was good to him. I hunted for work. I hunted every place and I couldn't find any kind of job. A recommendation from the pen don't help much."

"Go on, Matt," Robin said, her heart touched.

"When I saw all of you on the street in Pacific Point, I was pretty much shook up. I didn't know what to do. I'd hunted all around the peninsula for work as a cowhand. I like cows. I like horses. I even talked to old José, the *vaquero* at your ranch, Michael. He gave me some food, but no work. Hardtack Jack let me stay at his shack here for nothing. I'd just met Jeff at the bus station and we were on our way on foot to this place when we ran into that movie thing by mistake and saw the little girl and dog. We went on, got a lift a short ways to a place not far from the ranch. We were walking past it. It was about noon. There wasn't a soul around. I showed Jeff the palominos in the corral. He's crazy about horses the way I am. He wanted a ride. That was when I made my big mistake."

"You took Nugget!" Robin said, unbelieving.

"I didn't mean to." Matt's voice faltered. "I guess I just wanted to be a big shot in front of my kid, so I made up a story. I told him Nugget was my horse and of course he could have a ride. I didn't know his name, of course, but he came over and talked to me. Jeff sat on the fence and watched. He's some horse! I opened the gate and that horse came with me. Someone left a saddle across the corral fence, and I put it on to give Jeff a ride."

"Oh, dear, and I wanted so much to think you didn't steal Nugget," Robin said.

"I didn't," Matt insisted. "I only wanted to borrow him for about five minutes. Listen. We hadn't gone far, just to the edge of the field where the trail starts, when we ran into El Gato and Jake. I guess I talked too much in the pen about this cattle country. As soon as I saw them I knew what they were up to." His voice broke.

"Can't he wait to tell the rest?" Moira asked. "You only have to look at his bruised head. . . ."

"Thanks, but I want to go on. I *have* to go on. I didn't steal Nugget, did I, Jeff?"

"No, 'cause he was your horse!"

"He never was my horse, son. I'll have to try and explain that to you. I wish I didn't have to. Well, to go on. El Gato and Jake took the horse away from me. They held a gun on me till I got on Nugget, back of Jeff, and rode ahead of them. Jake was leading another cow pony. God only knows who'd ridden him before and what they'd done with him. Anyway, Jeff and I had to ride on."

"Where was Jeff when we saw you? He wasn't around," Robin said.

Matt jumped to his feet. "When *you* saw me? You saw me with El Gato?"

In a few words Robin and Mindy told Matt what they had seen and how they happened to see it.

"That was the *next* day," Matt said. "The day I met them they camped just below that mesa and got roaring drunk. When they passed out, I took Jeff and Nugget to Hardtack Jack's cabin. I told him not to let anyone come near the boy till I came back for them."

"Then what happened?" Kevin asked.

"I went back to El Gato and Jake. I knew if I didn't they'd hunt me down and kill both Jeff and me. I didn't help matters much by going back, the way things turned out. You saw me ride off with them, Robin . . . Mindy. You don't know what happened then. I'll tell you."

Robin pulled Jeff close to her, put her arm around him.

"We had gone about halfway down the mountain

when they stopped to talk. They'd found another use for me instead of loading calves. They held a gun to my back till they made me sign that bill of sale. I'd never have done it for myself. I wanted to live for my kid."

"Did they hurt you, Daddy?" Jeff cried. "Is that how you got hurt? Oh, Robin, they were awful bad men."

"They were that, all right," Matt agreed. "Say, do you suppose one of the girls could take Jeff to the shed out in back and get his things together? We'll be leaving soon, I hope."

Moira and Mindy, realizing that Matt didn't want to tell any more of his story in front of his boy, took Jeff with them.

"Thanks," he said. "He's a real man, that little guy, but I don't want him scared."

When they were gone, Matt went on.

"They tried to get rid of me then. We had stopped just at the edge of the bluff overlooking the river that rushes through the canyon. They jumped on me together, tied my arms and legs, and threw me over."

Robin gasped. "How awful! They meant to kill

you. They wanted to kill you, didn't they?"

"Yes. But they didn't. I hit a ledge. Because my clothes were ragged they caught on a scrub tree and held me up. I was knocked out. When I came to, it took me a long time to get the ropes loose, but I did it. Then I managed to climb up the cliff and start back here.

"You know the rest.

"What I want now is a chance to face El Gato and Jake. If you don't believe what I've told you, just watch their faces when they see me."

"That's the first thing we'll have to do," Robin said positively. "After we get Matt and Jeff to the ranch and have a doctor look after Matt, then he can talk to Sheriff Jackson. *I* believe he's telling the truth. I think Mindy believes he's telling the truth, too. You see, we heard him tell those men on the mesa that he didn't want to do anything wrong."

"I think he's a right guy, too, don't you, Kevin?" Michael said quickly.

"Yeah. He's had a bad deal, that's for sure. Do you think you can ride down the trail, Matt? If Robin rides Nugget that'll leave Bueno for you.

Think you can make it?"

"If I made it this far from the cliff on my own feet, it won't be hard to go the rest of the way on horseback. We can't get started too soon to suit me. How about old Hardtack Jack? Can't you let him go?"

"He's pretty ready with that gun. Let's go talk to him, Mike. You line up the rest of the gang to start back, will you, Robin?"

When they were ready to go, Robin on Nugget in the lead, with Jeff in the saddle with her, Hardtack Jack ran out of his shack to say good-bye. He was smiling. At least it seemed so, for his bushy beard had spread so his mouth could be seen.

"What caused all the change?" Robin turned to ask Michael, who rode back of her on Calico.

"Kev and I dug up a little loose change and gave it to him. We're friends now, but I wouldn't exactly say we're close friends, would you, Kev?"

"Nope. Who'd ever want to get that close to him?" Kevin made a face. "Say, it'll be dark, probably, before we can get to the ranch now. Lead on, Robin."

"Oh, I will! I can't wait to see everybody's faces

when we ride in with Nugget—and Matt!"

"I only wish the cameras would be turning," Moira said. "What a day! Who wants to be in a movie when real things like this happen?"

12. *Reward*

IT WAS STILL daylight when the cavalcade from Hardtack Jack's shack rode out of the fringe of forest and started across the field to the ranch.

Amy caught sight of them first. She was playing in the yard with Felipe and Judy.

"It's Nugget! Robin's riding Nugget!" she cried. "Mom! Daddy! José! Everybody! Just look who's coming across the field. Robin and Nugget!"

Heels flying, she ran to meet them. Felipe followed. Back of him little Judy hopped along. Tramp, barking joyfully, though he wasn't quite sure what it was all about, ran ahead. Fat old Perro, the ranch dog, left his wallow in the dust and geranium roots and waddled part way toward them, then lay down to wait.

Back of them came Robin's mother and father, Mr. Hunter, Tim Rafferty, José, and Mamacita calling out words of Spanish welcome and blessing.

"Hi, Robin!" Amy called breathlessly. "Where'd you find Nugget? Who's the boy with you?"

"Hi, Sugar! One question at a time." Robin reined in Nugget, slid off his back, and helped Jeff down. Back of her the others dismounted, all except Matt.

"The boy is Jeff," Robin told Amy. "Remember him? The little boy we saw on Roberto Street with his daddy when we were in the movie? Isn't it wonderful to have Nugget back?"

"Jeeminy, yes! Look, Judy, he's the same old Nugget!" Amy stroked the big horse's silvery mane. If a horse could be said to smile with contentment, Nugget did. He loved every bit of attention he had —Amy's petting, Judy's soft kiss on his long nose, even Tramp's *arf arf*.

When the older people caught up, Robin introduced Matt and quickly explained who he was and—

very briefly—how they had found him. "He's been hurt. He'll tell you all about that. I think we'd better ask the doctor to come out to look him over. Right now he needs to go to the bunkhouse for a shower and clean clothes. Then we'll get together and tell you the whole story. I guess you'll want Sheriff Jackson to be here at that time."

"Of course. I'll call him, Robin. I guess the team of Robin Kane and Mindy Hunter put one over on him, didn't they? In the nick of time, too, if it means keeping El Gato and Jake in custody."

"Robin did every bit of it. She followed the old man to the shack. Gol!" Kevin said. "Wait till the sheriff slaps an attempted murder charge against those two, in addition to rustling."

"Murder?" Mrs. Kane's face whitened in horror. "Whose murder? Oh, Robin!"

"Not mine. Matt's. Wait, though, till you hear the whole thing. Come to think of it, maybe we should have brought old Hardtack Jack along with us and held him under the same charge. That shotgun, you know."

"I think it's time for us to go on to the ranch house," Mr. Kane said soberly. "All this talk about murder and guns needs some explanation. Mamacita, here's another little *muchacho* for you to wash up and feed."

Mamacita beamed all over her kindly olive face. "I take him. Oh, there he go now, with Amy and Judy. Everybody go!" She made a shooing motion with her red calico apron. "Everybody hungry. Mamacita feed everybody."

Robin fell behind the others as they left, Nugget's reins in her hand. On the way she talked to him softly, soothingly, walking slowly at his side.

"Oh, Nugget, you darling, you're back with me again. I haven't had a chance to tell you how much I've missed you. Nothing will ever harm you again. Do you know what I'll do just as soon as we get to the barn?"

She put her mouth close to Nugget's listening ear. "I'll comb your beautiful coat very carefully. Till it's smooth and shiny again. There are burrs in your mane and tail. That's terrible. Then Nugget, dear, I'll give you some cool grain mash. I'll fix your clean straw bed and you can rest and rest. Come, Nugget! See the corral? You're back home!"

While Matt was showering, Robin and Mindy told

the others briefly what had occurred. When they had finished, their listeners' faces were grim. "Matt will explain the whole business in detail when the sheriff gets here," the girls concluded.

"It's a good thing for El Gato and Jake that they *are* in jail," Mr. Kane said, his fists clenched till the knuckles showed white. "When I think of you two girls at the mercy of those two murderers and that old man!"

"We weren't at their mercy, Daddy. They didn't see us on the mesa at all. Old Hardtack Jack's threats were all talk. Matt's the one who really suffered. Most of it is his story."

An hour later everyone had eaten dinner. Matt felt better after a good warm shower. He was anxious to get on to the business of El Gato and Jake. Jeff, washed and in some of Mamacita's grandson's clothes, played happily in the yard with Felipe, Amy, and Judy.

Sheriff Jackson arrived.

"Well, what you told me over the phone puts a different light on the bill of sale, doesn't it?" he asked. "Robin, you tell me your part of it first."

Robin shook her head. "Matt had better talk first. He'll burst if he doesn't. Those men were terribly cruel to him. I'll tell my part when he gets to where he was with El Gato and Jake on the mesa."

So Matt talked.

With various emotions, his listeners heard the whole grim story, clenching and unclenching their fists. Mrs. Kane's hand tightened on Robin's, her face drawn and shocked.

"So here I am," Matt concluded. "If Jeff hadn't made that drawing on the corral fence it's hard to tell what would have happened to me, and to Jeff. Robin has the making of an ace detective. How about it, Sheriff?"

"She's a fast worker, I'll say that. A couple of pretty hard specimens almost escaped. Where'd that tattoo come from, anyway, Matt? What does it mean?"

"It came from homesickness. When I was a kid and lived down in southern California, I played on the beach all day long. When dusk came I used to see the gulls in formation making for the rocks for the night. Then a long line of big pelicans would cross the sky, flying home. When I was in the army that was the picture that stood out in my mind—those pelicans against the dark blue sky. I had one tattooed on my arm. It seemed to keep me in touch with home."

"Later you lived up in this ranch country, didn't you?" Robin asked. "Jeff said he lived on a farm before you went to war."

"Yes. I was working as a cowhand on the J Bar X Ranch on the other side of the mountains. I'm crazy about horses—riding the range. Jeff's an old cowhand, too. Ten to one he's out there in the corral right now talking to the horses." Matt smiled proudly at the thought.

"I hate to break this up," the sheriff interrupted. "But we'd better get down to the county jail. You'll have to make a formal charge, Matt. Then I'll put those babies where they won't circulate for a while—or the judge will, when he hears what they've been up to. Mr. Hunter, you come, too, and Robin and Kevin and the other boy and girls. Let 'em see the whole kaboodle of you. It'll teach 'em that all good detectives don't wear guns on their hips and shoot up the countryside. They're sure in for a great big surprise."

When the story had been told again, and the men put away to wait trial, everyone gathered again at Rancho Lucia.

"Boy, did they ever wilt when they saw Matt!" Kevin told his father and mother and the others who had waited at the ranch. "You'd have thought they saw a monster from outer space! Say, that El Gato surely deserves his name. He's a wily one. Imagine trying to get away with that phony bill of sale."

"I'm glad the calves are all back in pasture," Matt said soberly. "Jake's no angel of mercy, either. He and El Gato are downright ornery. Those calves didn't have too good a time with them. And the horses! You should have seen how El Gato treated that pony of his."

"I did," Robin said quickly. "I saw how kind you were to the pony you rode, Matt. That was the first thing that made me pretty sure you couldn't have done the things the men said you did. A man who loves cows and horses—"

She paused suddenly. Her glance flew across the room to Mr. Hunter. He caught it and smiled.

"I know just exactly what you are thinking. It's

funny, I was thinking the same thing. Matt, I could use another good hand on the ranch. How about it?"

Matt put his head down on his arms. He couldn't answer.

Jeff could. "Then we can stay here all the time? We can live here all the time? With Felipe? And Mamacita? And José? And my daddy's horse?"

"Right you are about the first things, Jeff," Mr. Hunter answered. "Mamacita will like to have another little *muchacho* to mother, won't you?"

Mamacita's smiling face was answer enough. José, listening, clapped his hands and Jeff ran and jumped into his lap.

"You're wrong about the last thing, Jeff," Mr. Hunter continued. "You and Felipe and Amy and Judy . . . well, you kids can claim all the other horses you want to claim on the ranch. But Nugget is different."

"Yes, son. I told you he never really was my horse. I just pretended and that's what caused all the trouble," Matt said, regret in his voice.

"I forgot," Jeff said. "Felipe said I could name Nugget's colt. I think I'll call him 'Pelican'!"

"That's a good enough name," Mr. Hunter agreed.

"A very good name. As I said, Nugget is different. I have other plans for him."

He reached into his pocket and took out a folded paper. "Pass this over to Robin, please, Michael."

Wide-eyed, Robin read:

> "I do hereby transfer all right and ownership of a palomino horse called 'Nugget,' now registered in my name, to Robin Kane, to have and to hold forever.
>
> Signed: Maxfield Hunter."

Her voice shaking with wonder, Robin asked, "Honest? Cross your heart? Nugget is *my* horse?"

"Cross my heart!" Mr. Hunter said and drew an X across his breast. "It's a two-way love affair between you and Nugget. He wants to be your horse, Robin. He's really never been anything else. We'll keep him here at the ranch for you as long as you want us to. It's very little reward for the return of my calves. I'm grateful for that. It was a smart job. Nugget is yours, honey."

With a rush, Robin crossed the room, threw her arms around Mr. Hunter and hugged him tight.

Then, her face radiant with happiness, she held the paper high in her hand, skipped across the room and opened the door.

"I've got to go and tell Nugget," she said. "I think he'll be glad, too."